HARMONY

Copyright © 2025 Flash Kitterson
Cover Illustration: Cogtypelawbot

ISBN: 978-1-965229-01-9 (Paperback)

PROLOGUE

Deep amidst the infinite, uncharted plains of the unknown, there was a land of plenty. Full to the brim with flourishing fauna and flora, painted in all possible shades by vivid, fertile climates, and populated by anthropomorphic animals and humans alike.

Ophin, the god of destiny, created both this land and its people, and spent the succeeding eons watching over them with great care, tact, and satisfaction. As he did, the minds of the people and their societies grew wise, diverse, and strong – bringing about a long golden age of might and magic.

Yet, as is true amidst every great era, there remained forgotten corners of shadow. Even as the kingdoms and their bustling domains blossomed – great, noble Penlight amongst them – there remained a few outlying settlements where the gilded lights of innovation or prosperity rarely touched. Where kinship and goodwill were fickle havens at best, and brutish forces of might and cunning reigned above all.

It was in one of these villages, lodged between the face of a hard, cold range of mountains and the sea, that two cheetahs lived in a derelict church long since abandoned by those of Ophin's faith. The pair were named Ren and Seiichi – father and son, and the only surviving family of their late wife and mother.

Ren had taken his lover's death like a blade through the very heart – sinking to the drink and long, long nights alone in the cemetery of her final rest with an absolute abandon that saw him grow thin and matted, and completely snuffed out the once stalwart pride with which he had tended to his home, village, and family.

Seiichi had not remained unscathed either, and not just in terms of his own grief. For Ren felt pain anytime he saw his son. It was his name and his eyes – both so vividly like hers. And so he struck out at that cruelly familiar face almost daily – berating it with cruel, hateful words til Seiichi could do little more other than cower and weep, and at times striking it literally with his fists and claws.

This continued for season upon season with no sign of stopping, or possible hope that Ren's all-consuming sorrow and hatred towards himself, the world, or his son would grow less over time.

Continued, until the third anniversary of Seiichi's mother's passing – when Seiichi's life changed forever, and the land took its first step in a long, winding cycle of change that would utterly transform history forevermore.

The sky above the graveyard and touching the never-ending length of unruly sea beyond its rocky borders was thick was tumultuous grey – fitting for the occasion, and matching the plain-spun garb worn by the sole two figures amongst those stones. Seiichi knelt before the barely adorned, weed-decked of his mother, mouthing silent prayers under his breath, and kneading his thumbs in his tightly-clasped hands. Ren stood behind him – straight-backed, empty-faced, and with his arms folded before his lower chest.

They had been posed there for longer than Seiichi could gauge – perhaps hours – and had not traded a single word for even longer. Seiichi had no way of knowing for how many more hours their vigil would continue, but he too was consumed by grief in his own way to care, and knew better than to interrupt his father's stoic, almost mindless trance of anger-tinged reflection to ask.

Despite the dense, heavy stone of emotion deep in Seiichi's gut and the prickling in his green eyes, this wariness also kept him from sobbing out loud. But not from feeling utterly, crushing lonely. The first years had been tolerable, back when Ren had wept instead of screamed and raged. He had had at least some comfort to offer to his son, and the weight of loss had felt like a burden they were bearing together. But now... that father was gone. Ren was a parent no more, and in his place was a bitter vindicative monster.

That last thought was too much, even given his fear-steeled composure. Completely of their own accord, tears began to flow from Seiichi's eyes, and down onto his pressed hands. At first they were silent, but then his back heaved and a miserable gasp for air escaped from between his lips.

That was enough. Seconds after, Seiichi could hear his father shifting somewhat behind him, undoubtedly moving to stare down with a steely scowl. "You know better than to cry, Seiichi."

Seiichi stopped praying, and his body tensed up with reflexive fear at the darkness in Ren's tone. He dared not raise his head to look back, however – knowing without any sliver of a doubt that showing the visual evidence of his tears would earn him a strike across the face. "It's hard to stop, father."

A moment of silence followed, in which the boy hoped fervently that his father would spare him a scolding and continue to mourn in frigid peace, but then a firm hand descended upon the scruff of his neck in an instant – hauling him to his feet and to face his father with a strength that caused his entire spine to scream in pain. The last time he had seen it, Ren's face had been expressionless and limp, as it usually was these days. But now it was stretched in an almost grotesque manner – muzzle wide and teeth bared with raw, terrible anger.

"Hard?" The rough-furred cheetah almost spat with the fury behind his words. "What would you, runt, know of hard things? Of having all good in life stripped away? Of being left with the sad, sick leftovers of a failed legacy?"

Moving again far quicker than Seiichi could reckon with, Ren lashed out with a firm blow to his son's muzzle with his free hand – sending the boy stumbling back and almost tripping over a dead tree stump to the side of his mother's grave. Even then as he struggled to regain his footing and cradled at his face, however, he avoided making a single sound or meeting his father's eyes, so terrified he was of feeding the flames of his volatile fury further.

Thankfully, Ren didn't advance upon his son after that first blow, and instead turned from him to face back towards his wife's grave as though he simply couldn't bear to look upon Seiichi any longer. "Enough of this pathetic nonsense.

Your prayers insult her spirit." He bowed his head, and arched up his shoulders. "Go. Now. I want to be alone with her."

Seiichi dared not hesitate in obeying, even as he cradled the stinging pain of his father's merciless strike. Turning on his heel, the boy stepped away and began to make across the graveyard with a stumbling pace that soon turned to a desperate, disorientated run. His sobbing broke back out as soon as he left his father's sight, and continued at full volume until he left the dead orchard that ringed the landbound side of the graveyard and arrived back at the towerless, derelict church that they called 'home'.

Vines clawed at the building's stone sides, and what of its ornate wood decorations that remained were rotted and broken – including the frame of the small, doorless side entryway through which Seiichi stumbled through now. One turn left through the dark, thin stone corridor beyond, and he arrived at the modest, ragged cloth-hammocked space which served as his own quarters. The ceiling here had stones missing, and the wall opposite his makeshift bed was lined by a tall stained glass window that had likely used to have been brilliant and gleaming.

No sooner had the cheetah boy moved inside than he collapsed – first to his knees. and then to an awkward, folded sit – pressing his hands back together, shutting his eyes, and beginning to pray once more, this time making no effort to keep the tears from falling or his sobs from echoing through the hollow building.

His thoughts were solely occupied by making the same desperate pleas to Ophin again and again – his only possible defense against the darkness and despair welling up within him on days like this.

Seiichi felt closest to his mother when praying to Ophin. She had been a devout follower, although Ren had never fully approved of her faith, and their times prostate together before the church's modest altar – which Ren had long since smashed and removed from the building – remained some of his dearest memories.

She always told me that Ophin decides your destiny. The young cheetah furrowed his brow, forcing his tears to stem for a moment. *Is my destiny to die by my father's paws?*

At times, Seiichi truly believed that it would happen. One day, not so far in the future. The way that Ren looked at him grew darker each time – each glance carrying with it a depth of intent and flickering, irrational thought behind it that shook Seiichi to his very soul. He'd heard his father say it out loud once, too – whispered about a threshold in the church during one of his regular bouts of agitatable isolation. *May as well end this for good. All of this.*

Just then a creaking sound echoed from somewhere within the church, and Seiichi's heart and head jolted up in fear. But no footsteps followed – only a burst of particularly chilly air – and his expression soon sunk back down in sorrow. Not father. Not yet.

Now that his eyes had raised, however, Seiichi noticed something out of the ordinary. The space around him was... brighter, somehow. The weather outside had been grey and wet without reprieve for weeks, as befitted the season, and he had seen nothing during their vigil outside to indicate that that would be changing anytime soon, but the longer that he stared up at the colors of the window through his tear-blurred eyes, the brighter and more vibrant they appeared to grow, until he was forced to squint and bring his paw in front of his eyes.

This was not sufficient – as before long the light appeared to cling to the tawny fur of his very paw, until it was at first almost as if and then undeniable that the shine was coming *from* him, rather than shining upon him.

At first Seiichi was simply awestruck, but then... he suddenly came to understand. Divinity was at play here. His prayers had finally been answered. "This is part of the destiny Ophin gave me, isn't it?" The cheetah boy held out his paw, squinting hard against the sharp luminescence raining down upon him and radiating from his paw.

Yet even as he said those incredulous, awed words, he knew that it was more than that. More than destiny. New thoughts flooded his mind, and with them a hope and gleam that had been absent within him since his mother's death – the realization that he was no longer powerless and waiting for a sign, and that he could do anything. That he could not only fulfill a bright destiny in the name of Ophin, but *change* his destiny.

Above all, he knew exactly, down to every miniscule detail, what he had to do next.

Another echo sounded through the stones of the church, and this time he *did* hear footsteps signifying his father's entry into the building, but the young cheetah no longer felt trepidation as a result. Instead, a tired but relieved smile slowly crept across his face as he stared down at his newfound light.

Ideas, ambitions, and sparks of realization shot through his head. Almost without any conscious decision, he found himself leaning over on his knees and scrabbling about with both hands in the corner of the space – searching blindly until his fingers changed upon a jagged, arm-length piece of hardwood. Next, he began to cautiously step out of his room and down the church's hall in the direction of his father's movements.

"Seiichi." His father's voice boomed between the stones. "You will fetch me bread. Then I will continue my vigil. Be quick, and silent."

The cheetah boy didn't respond, and instead continued slowly advancing down the hall with the small stake behind his back. At that moment, however, Ren came about the doorway directly across from him – stopping in the very center of the threshold, and immediately bringing his dangerous eyes to bear upon his son.

Yet where the sight of his father standing so commandingly before him would have sent a jolt of cold dread to Seiichi's stomach before, it gave him little pause now. The boy continued to approach instead of moving to obey – shifting closer and closer with his hands still behind his back.

Ophin will guide me.

Soon he was directly before Ren – the older male towering over him and arching his brow in angry confusion. "Why do you not obey, boy? Do not test me. What do you have behind your back?"

One last long, steadying breath, and he acted. Raising his right paw as quickly as he could, he gritted his fangs hard, and cried out loud. "Shine!"

The light in his palm had been glowing dully this entire time, but now it flared unbelievably, supernaturally bright – causing Ren to first blink, then stagger back in pain and shock with a sharp hiss. "What the- the hell!?"

Seiichi's left hand acted next. Summoning every inch of strength from throughout his frame, the cheetah boy clenched the stake hard, and thrust if forward from his side directly towards his father's chest without a moment's hesitation.

The blow stuck perfectly true, and the makeshift weapon pierced through the cloth and flesh on Ren's chest with almost surreal ease.

All was silent for a moment, aside from the powerful thudding in Seiichi's ears, the humming of energy radiating from his still-glowing paw, and a single, rattling gasp from Ren.

What played out next happened almost as though in slow motion. Ren began to crumble to his knees. The boy pulled his arm back, unsheathing the stake from his father's chest. And, now unsupported, the older cheetah slumped over completely with a dull thud.

Ren didn't say anything. Or perhaps he couldn't. He simply laid there where he had fallen – staring up with wide, shocked eyes even as his lips opened and closed soundlessly, and a pool of rich blood blossomed out onto the mossy church stones around him.

Seiichi too said nothing as his father continued to struggle and twitch – allowing the stake to fall and staring down at the shaking, bloody paw that had been holding it. The brilliance of his fingers still flickered and pulsed with Ophin's radiance, but he barely noticed anymore. His entire world had shrunk to the crimson stain spreading beneath his father's body and the sickly, rattling breaths issuing from Ren's throat.

The man who had tormented him. The man who had beaten and berated him. The man who had cursed his very existence.

The glow in Seiichi's palm finally dimmed to its earlier, mild glow, as though the god's presence had withdrawn in silent acknowledgment of what had transpired. A final benediction? A test?

Ren's mouth opened one last time. His eyes – so often cold, so often cruel – were different now. They held something else. Not hate. Not rage. But recognition.

His lips parted. A whisper, barely audible over the wind outside and the thudding in Seiichi's ears. "Nara..."

His mother's name. Ren's wife.

Then the cheetah's chest fell still, body slumping into stillness. His eyes remained open, locked upon the rafters above them.

Seiichi's breath came in sharp, shallow gulps. He staggered back, and his heel caught on the uneven stones – sending him tumbling onto his backside. He barely noticed the pain. His entire body felt numb, and his mind weightless. *I did it. It's.... over.*

His mother had told him that Ophin wove the fates of all, that no action – no matter how great or small – was beyond the god's watchful eye. Had this been ordained from the start? Had the god, in the end, merely given him the means to fulfill what had always been written? Or had he chosen? Had he taken fate into his own hands?

Despite the deep morbidity of the sight, despite the sharp scent of blood now suffusing his nostrils... the boy felt no sadness, nor grief, nor fear that his sudden, violent deed would be discovered or condemned. Tears began to fall from Seiichi's eyes, but not of sorrow – accompanied, rather, by a smile. A wide grin like no other that he had given for three long, cold years.

"Thank you, Ophin. Thank you!"

Shifting to his knees and continuing to gratefully weep, the boy began to pray next to his father's body in a deep trance – for the first time feeling thankful not only for the comfort that Ophin afforded him, but also for the power that he could still feel coursing through his body and fingertips. That had allowed him to seize hold of his destiny.

Some time later, the young cheetah wiped his tears away, rose, and crept over to the church door. With his heart almost beating out of his chest, he looked around, saw no one nearby in the grey shrubbery outside, and made back over to his father's corpse. His left hand, sticky with warmth that was not his own, grasped Ren's arms and dragged them into place – folded across his chest as if in mock prayer.

The weight of the body was immense, but his resolve outweighed it. Step by step, he hooked his hands beneath his father's shoulders, gritted his teeth, and pulled.

The body scraped against the stone, leaving a dark trail in its wake. Ren had been heavy in life, but in death, he felt like an anchor trying to drag Seiichi down with him. The young cheetah's muscles screamed, his back ached, but he did not stop. He moved past the broken pews, past the altar his father had shattered long ago, past the light filtering through the stained glass that had first ignited his awakening.

By the time he reached the back entrance, Seiichi's body burned from exertion, but he felt none of it. The graveyard was waiting. There was no stopping now.

Seiichi pulled Ren's body across the damp earth, past the old gravestones weathered by time and neglect, past the overgrown weeds that had swallowed so many forgotten names. And then, at last, he reached the place where it had all begun. His mother's crumbling, weed-covered grave.

Seiichi let go, and Ren's body slumped onto the grass beside it. His father – who had spent years desecrating her memory with his hate – would now spend eternity beside her.

He dropped to his knees, his chest rising and falling with slow, deliberate breaths. His paws dug into the soil. There was no hesitation. No second thoughts. He would bury his father here. With his own hands, if he had to.

And when it was done, he would plan to leave this place. Forever.

Hours later, with the red of sunset beginning to dye the clouds on the horizon, Seiichi returned to the church – making through its courtyard until he came to the building's half-collapsed front, facing out onto the village road ahead. A few decrepit houses lined the way, and in the near distance he could see the foot of the mountain at the settlement's edge looming over them.

Slowly sitting down on the broken steps that led down in front of the doors, the cheetah boy let out a long, deep breath, and leaned his head back against the wood behind him.

In these few moments, his life had changed in ways that he could not possibly imagine – that much he knew already – but could nonetheless feel in every cell of his body. The inspiration within him had not faded, banishing every corner of the melancholy and hopelessness that had filled him for so many years, and that upon his paw hadn't either – still visible even out here in the weak, grey sunlight.

Bemused, Seiichi slowly waved his right paw about in the air – trailing its light out in colorful, illusory waves that caught his eye and fascinated him to no end. *Leftovers no more. Look what I can do, father.*

"What are you doing?"

The voice, high and lilting, tore the cheetah boy's eyes away from his glowing paw and upwards to see a black-furred, grey-eyed cat girl standing not a few feet away from him with her head tilted inquisitively – somewhat difficult to make out amongst the grey around them and the fading light from the sky above in her own rough-spun clothes.

Seiichi's heart pounded faster as he stared at her, and she moved her blonde hair out of her eyes with her paw. He didn't know what to say.

The silence between them extended for a few moments, before the cat girl gestured to Seiichi's paw. "Your paw. It's doing something."

The boy couldn't help but let his eyes dart back to the light for a moment to follow her pointing, briefly seeing its color fade from white to a bright pink, and then – slowly – fade altogether.

Despite the fact that the light was gone and his paw was back to normal, Seiichi nonetheless hid it in his lap – next to his left paw, which was still somewhat stained by blood. "It's... nothing." Next he tilted his own head. "But who are you?"

The question was an attempt to redirect the girl's attention, but a genuine one nonetheless. He hadn't ever seen her in the village, and the coast's population was far too thin for him not to have met her already.

Ears perking a little, the girl gave a short, awkward kind of curtsy that was almost funny to Seiichi. "I'm Tsuki Mei – from the Penlight Kingdom. I'm visiting my grandmother here. And who are you?"

"I'm Sei..." The boy stopped himself, choked midway through his name. He couldn't bring himself to say it, after all the times that his father had uttered it in anger. After how tightly Ren had tied it to the significance of his failure as a son. *No. I will forsake it, just like a true faithful of Ophin would. From now on I will be known for the magic that saved me, and what I can do.*

"Illusionary," he finally answered. "My name is Illusionary."

Tsuki tilted her head. "Illusionary? That's a curious name."

Illusionary nodded. *So it is. But so is also the destiny that Ophin has laid out before me, and that I have chosen to mold.*

"My grandmother lives there." Changing the subject, the girl pointed to the house across from the church. "Where do you live? Why are you out in front of the church?"

That stumped the cheetah boy, and he could only blink for a few moments. "I don't know. I don't live anywhere, for now. And... I'm guess I'm just... waking up."

That appeared to again confuse the other feline, but before she could speak more, an older womanly voice came from somewhere along the rough road behind her. "Tsuki! Come back inside! Supper's ready."

"Oh." Tsuki sighed, and turned slightly on her heel. "I have to go. Hopefully we'll talk again sometime soon?"

Illusionary nodded and started to wave in farewell, but the girl had already started to dash away before he could even properly raise his paw. Nonetheless, he watched raptly after her grey tail until she vanished up into the threshold of the small house from which the voice had come earlier.

Eventually, when she had been gone for some time, he exhaled and put his chin to his paw. He liked this new girl, almost as much as he liked the infinite range of possibilities that his new freedom and power had opened up before him.

Those thoughts made Illusionary smile, and bow his head in prayer once more. *Thank you, Ophin.*

Your destiny – our destiny – is beautiful. And so, so full of potential.

Months later, during the spring, Tsuki returned home to her home at the edge of the Penlight Kingdom – a village nestled in the curving breast of a river, and surrounded by plains that spanned far and wide in swathes of golden farmland to the west, all the way to the walls of Penlight Castle itself.

Although his interactions with Tsuki herself rarely went beyond observantly watching the girl from the shadows, Illusionary followed her – bound to neither his old home, his mother's old home, nor the church by anything more than soured memories and half-buried, stripping bones.

It was there that he found a new home in the hubris of the Kingdom – a brighter, kinder place than anything he had ever known – taking on chores and errands for the village church in exchange for his keep, and Tsuki met a mild-mannered white cat of her age named Daku.

Daku was the son of the merchant who delivered foodstuffs to her parents, and as such their first meetings were irregular and determined wholly by those business dealings. Soon, however, they began to meet with one another of their own accord – spending long afternoons and evening talking, and fresh mornings exploring the dense wilderness that surrounded the eastern side of the village.

On one such expedition, upon a particularly spectacular day, the pair sat upon a log together – gazing out at the glade of gently swaying trees surrounding them, and listening closely to the flow of the river in the near distance just beyond.

Tail swaying, and hands clasped in the lap of her light cotton blouse, Tsuki turned to Daki with a gentle, encouraging smile. "You know, you don't talk about yourself often."

Nervous, but bearing a smile of his own, Daku shifted his muzzle to the side a little before answering. "I don't know... I guess I don't think there's that much to say. I mean, I enjoy reading, relaxing, and nature. It's why I like coming out here so much." He inched his paw closer to hers along the log, although he dared not raise his eyes while doing so. "What about you?"

Tsuki's eyes lit up. "The same things, really! Except..." They dulled again, and her face fell sharply. "My parents didn't use to let me outside that often. Going out with you... is the first time I've been able to visit the forest so often."

Daku frowned – a little concerned at the change in the girl's voice. "Why? Why would they do that?"

Tsuki's face and head stayed downcast – the balance between them completely upended in terms of shyness. "Because of my powers, I suppose."

The male cat's frown turned incredulous, though in a somewhat excited way. "Powers?"

"Yeah!" Seeming a little emboldened by Daku's apparent lack of trepidation, Tsuki smiled and raised one of her paws. Soon, though the male cat could not believe his eyes, a dark aura began to surround it and emanate from her paw digits – coming directly from them, though in a mystical, almost blurry way that he couldn't quite make out or even begin to understand.

Daku's eyes widened in awe, though he remained still and sitting, and didn't move his own paw back across the log. "Wow... that's like nothing I've... ever seen before..." He blinked up at her. "Have you always been able to do that?"

"I think so – ever since I was born! Well, that's what my Mom told me, at least..." She swirled her paw digits around, watching the darkness curl about her wrist. "Although my parents told me not to use them too much. Does it scare you?"

Daku frowned incredulously and shook his head. "Not at all! It's amazing. Is like the queen's knights – they have powers too, you know, with things like ice, fire, and air."

"Really?" Tsuki meowed, and her tail lashed. That sounded exciting – she'd lived here all her life, but her parents had never told her that there were others like her out there at all, let alone so near. *Perhaps I can become one of them, someday.* "I thought you might not want to talk to me anymore if I showed you."

The other cat chuckled. "Some see light in the darkness, you know."

Tsuki's eyes drifted downwards, and it was her, now, who had a nervous blush spreading across her cheeks. "You're... so sweet." She waved her paw in the air, and the darkness upon it formed in the air in what was soon apparent to be a heart shape.

"See? This isn't scary," he said – watching the energy and trailing out around them with an awestruck expression. "This is beautiful."

"T-thank you... I'm glad you think so!" She lowered her paw and smiled shyly.

For a long while they simply sat there in silence – watching the remnants of Tsuki's energy fan out around them in peace.

Yet, suddenly and without warning, it seemed almost as though the tendrils extending out towards the roof of the glade were growing – expanding and splitting wider like cracks in the very air. Before long, both Daku and Tsuki scrambled to their feet – waving their arms about in a fruitless attempt to clear them like spiderwebs, and swiftly becoming blinded by the enveloping dark.

Daku – feeling his vision giving out altogether, almost as though he had completely lost control of his eyes – reached out his arms and floundered about in hopes of finding something, anything to grab onto. "Tsuki?! Where are you? I can't see anything."

Tsuki's voice just barely reached his ears in response. "I can't see anything either. What's happening?!"

The male cat opened his muzzle to respond, but that turned out to be a grave mistake. No sooner had his lips parted than a thick, intrusive force pried its way inside – stifling Daku's resulting scream, and sending him staggering back. Yet, even as his feet tripped up and he went tumbling, there was no ground, and there was no impact – only falling, falling, swirling, and...

Nothing.

Tsuki woke up first – eyes blinking open for one second, before squinting shut in the second after as she processed the discomfort of her back and legs laying flat on the hard forest ground.

Nothing made sense. She could remember... disorientation and the swirling dark, but that was what a nap felt like, sometimes, no?

When her eyes opened, she saw the sun and the roof of the forest glade above her, and a somewhat panicked glance to her side revealed Daku laying next to her – also on his back, muzzle pointed upwards, and eyes closed.

"Ugh... I don't remember what I was doing." The female cat pulled herself slowly to her knees, before leaning over and shaking Daku by the shoulders. "I hope you're okay..."

She expected him to jerk back awake, but instead he merely yawned and stretched – eyes slowly blinking open in a groggy fashion. "T-tsuki? I'm so tired. Haven't we explored enough for today? I don't want to fall asleep again out here."

Tsuki frowned a little at this, but did see some logic in his words, and as such nodded cautiously. *That must be it. And we haven't had anything to eat, either.* "Sure thing."

At that, they stood up and dusted themselves off as one, and took one another's hand – weaving through the trees back to their village as though nothing had happened, and with only the day's fare on their minds.

Yet, at that moment, beyond the narrow span of their awareness, a long line of fate had been irrevocably set into motion.

A line that was as cruel as it was essential for the future of the Penlight Kingdom and all of Ophin's land beyond it, and as lined in tragedy and pain as it was in hope, greatness, and destiny.

Ten years later

Penlight Castle could not possibly have been described as anything less than a spire of stately authority and majestic beauty – stood over the many-tiered rings of its walled outskirts as though it were Ophin's crown, and the golden fields surrounding them his flowing hair. At the castle's center, set high in its peak like the jewel of that crown, stood the queen's palace – the royal residence, the rallying point of the Knights of Penlight, and the seat of the kingdom's governance.

With the sun stood high in the sky, folk flowed in and out of the palace's sandstone gates with swarm-like regularity. Amongst them were tradespeople delivering their goods and services with packs and tools in hand, common folk strolling at their own leisure, and delegations from the towns and villages upon official business.

Within the inner courtyard of the palace, where the light of the day was diffused by the walls and the colorful banners upon them, the pace and volume of things were at least somewhat more reserved. With the exception, notably, of a single rich, proud voice that stemmed from the muzzle of a devout, impassioned servant.

That devout servant was Illusionary – stood upon a wooden step to raise his gold, spotted head above the crowd, the white robe of a priest set across his shoulders, and sermon upon his lips.

"Ophin creates our destiny. We must accept it – for he gave us our lives, and seeks to guide us to glory within them."

The cheetah clenched his paw in the air, scanning the half-flowing, half-static mass of faces spread out before him with his green eyes wide. In those that stood still and were truly listening... he could see hope. Belief. Faith. And that brought a deep burst of joy. *Yes, they will finally know your glory. Hear me preach your word!*

Letting the fresh, passionate energy flow from his veins to his arms, he raised his right paw high, and released a burst of glittering white energy out in the air of the square in front of him. Illusionary's smile grew as noises of excitement from the crowd echoed in his ears. Feet stopped, heads turned, and jaws dropped. Reveling at the peak of their attention, he put his paws together and closed his eyes. "Live in his strength – feel his guidance."

That had the crowd distracted and chattering amongst themselves for a few moments, and in that time, the robed cheetah stole a glance over his shoulder at the pair of figures nestled to one side of the tall, open wooden doors some distance across the stones behind him. One, a black furred female cat in the robes of a Knight of Penlight, and the second a slightly taller white-furred male in common dress. Tsuki, and her *dear* lover Daku.

Oh, Tsuki... The rapturous smile failed to fade from Illusionary's lips, but his thoughts were bitter – more disappointed than sad or even jaded. *What happened to you? The beauty of your youth... Wasted. A shame, but so are things, I suppose.*

Tsuki's own thoughts, however, could not have been more different. She had fallen deaf to Illusionary's sermons long ago, just as she was utterly unaware of his eyes on her now. For now, all that she saw and all that she cared for was the golden glow of the sunlight in Daku's white fur.

He, unlike Tsuki herself, was not a knight of the kingdom, but taking over his father's business as a deliveryman did occasionally allow him to ferry goods to the palace and slip by his lover while she was on duty. This visit, however, was vastly different from their usual affairs. The talk between them was far more sincere, and sincerity was written across the male feline's face.

"I don't know about this..." Finally caving to a frown, Daku rubbed at the back of his head. "What if they end up having powers too, and have a hard time controlling them? Are we really equipped to deal with something like that?"

"They'll have their mother, father, and the knights to help them!" Tsuki meowed and rubbed Daku's shoulders. "I trust them to know what to do, and to help us. Just like I trust you." She kissed her lover on the forehead.

He ruffled a little at the kiss, although he didn't appear reluctant to receive it. "And I trust you too. But your powers... are something else altogether, at times. I think my reasons for worrying are justified."

She sighed and reached down to take hold of his paw. "But they aren't something else. They are part of me. And if you trust me too, if you love me... Then you already know all that you need to."

He looked away and took a deep, steadying breath. "I'm sorry, you're right. I'm just being... cautious."

"Daku..." The enthusiasm in her face softened, and her grip tightened around his hands. "I'll be fine, and the kitten will be fine, too. Now, will you stop worrying?"

He sighed again, and finally glanced back to meet her eyes – squeezing back against her grip on his paw now. "Then I trust you, Tsuki. We can try for a child."

Smiling wider than he thought he'd ever seen her before, Tsuki pulled him in for a kiss and closed her eyes. Daku's own eyes remained open for a moment, but then he closed them too, and lost himself in their closeness and the warmth of the sun upon them.

Maybe everything would be alright after all. The kingdom was strong, the knights were wise, and Tsuki... was everything that he'd ever wished for and more.

They remained like this for some time, embracing tightly with no regard for the public shifting about them. Illusionary's sermons picked back up – drowning on and on as the sun drifted lower in the sky, and the lovers whispered half-sincere plans for the future.

The months turned to a year, as the days grew shorter and then longer again, and the seasons cycled from winter back to bloom.

As the spring was born, so was Daku and Tsuki's daughter – brought to the world in their house in the villages surrounding Penlight Castle's sprawl. Tsuki did not suffer long from the throes of birth, nor did she wail or cry from its pains and exertions. The child's body was fully gray, but the fur on her face was white on the left and gray on the right.

Tsuki chose to call her daughter Harmony. Harmony Mei.

Yet while Daku was quickly swept in parental bliss across the days that followed, and all his previous doubts quickly subsided, the detachment and relative emotionlessness that Tsuki had exhibited during the birth only deepened. She would hold the child with no expression upon her face, and rise and rest with the mornings and evenings without engaging in more than the barest minimum of conversation.

Daku was confused and distressed by this jarring change at first, but soon came to rationalize worry away – he had heard that an adjustment period and emotional turmoil was common amongst new mothers, after all, and as long as the child and Tsuki herself were physically sound… surely, nothing else mattered.

Once she was fully recovered, Tsuki was quick to declare that she wished to return to service amongst the knights and the kingdom, to which Daku responded with cautious optimism. The first week of her duties passed without event, but even by the eighth day, the male cat had still been unable to completely shake his worry.

Upon that morning, Daku stood in their hall with Harmony in his arms, watching his wife change into her leather uniform. She had yet to speak a word to him since they had woken together, as was uncomfortably common these days, and remained silent even after finishing up with the fastening of her chest piece and moving to unlatch the door.

"Are you sure you're fine, darling?" he questioned, before she could shift through.

Tsuki just barely glanced over her shoulder. "Yes." She sighed. "I'm fine, it's just work. Be back later."

Then she was walking past the threshold into the sun of the outside, pausing on the first of the cobblestones of the village road, and vanished in a burst of black smoke – leaving Daku standing framed by the threshold of the house with a deep, worried frown upon his face.

Manifesting amidst a dense burst of black arcane fog, Tsuki appeared within the inner walls of Penlight Palace – stood upon the straight stone path that lead directly through the well-tended lawns to the inner sanctum's entrance. There were two guards posted to either side of the threshold in front of her, but they bowed and lowered their halberds as the feline moved forward at a brisk pace.

They weren't alone, however. Leaning against the wall behind the two armored men was a human male with brown hair, a white button-up shirt, and brown pants – Mase Yaketsuku, another of the Knights of Penlight, and in control of magical fire.

Mase raised his head as Tsuki drew near, and pushed away from the wall. "You're here early," he commented, tilting his head to the side mockingly and widening his blue eyes to greet her.

"The early bird catches the worm, Mase." Tsuki spat back, barely moving her head to glance at him as she stormed past.

The human knight blinked in surprise at her cold mannerisms as she brushed by, before pushing away from the wall and moving to follow her with a tsk and another quip. "Aren't you a cat?"

The stone arches widened and the final threshold to the throne room approached, and yet Tsuki neglected to turn about. "Hilarious."

The two remained silent as the hall beyond enveloped them. Within it were more banners, more ornate furniture, and centermost among it all, a grand, wooden throne. As picturesque as it was, however, it could not hope to compare to the figure sat upon it – a golden, almost fiery-furred hound with a soft, white silk across her shoulders and chest, piercing eyes, and flowing hair that came long past her thin arms. Upholder – the Queen.

Next to the hound woman and her throne was a buck with short, brown hair and a wooden staff that curved at the top – the Queen's personal guard, Kijury Weathers – and before the two stood Illusionary. The cheetah was wearing the white and gold-edged robes of high priest – a station to which he had been promoted earlier in the year.

The two new arrivals were soon within speaking range of the rest, and could hear Illusionary's voice rising in falling gently in the Queen's ear – at which Mase scoffed out loud. "I see we're just in time for the church's newest round of begging and hoarding."

Glancing back over his shoulder with an incredulous look, the high priest moved his gaze from Tsuki to Mase with scathing intensity. "I'll have you know that the affairs of the church are the affairs of the people."

Mase rolled his eyes at this, but now it was the queen's turn to speak – giving a long, tired sigh and shaking her head of long hair before raising a voice that was as rich and bronzed as her fur. "I would appreciate avoiding any such interruptions in the future, Mase."

The fire knight and Tsuki came to stand to attention along the chamber's left wall, opposite the three figures stood likewise on the other side. All were dressed in the same service leathers as Mase and Tsuki herself, but their appearances were as widely varied as could be.

One – Mystic Shimizu – was a human woman with blue hair, and next to her was another taller, stronger human woman with blonde hair – Ika Raiden. On Ika's right stood an even taller, hooded man with a neutral mental mask, crooked horns, and long brown cloths covering his head and neck. Yuuto Touma.

For a while they stood in silence listening to Illusionary's speech, but it wasn't long before Mase took another jab at Tsuki – although he made a point of looking away from her as he did so. "I can't believe you're back at work already. Bored of the baby?"

That snapped something in the cat's demeanor. "Enough about my child!"

With a furious, sharp push, she shoved at Mase – causing him to stagger back away from her into the center of the throne room, and a shocked silence to fall throughout the space.

Next, she hunched down threateningly as, after he regained his balance with an affronted grunt, Mase fell back into a fighting stance of his own, and his hands gathered flames.

Mystic almost started forward with diplomatic intent, but then her eyes flared with fear at the sight of Tsuki's dark aura growing stronger and stronger, and she froze still. "Tsuki, calm yourself. We've talked about this."

That only stoked Tsuki's apparent rage, and caused her to bristle further. "Don't act as though you care about me," she growled. "All you ever talk about is the child. To my face, and behind my back." The cat scoffed and spat. "Muttering, whispering... more and more voices. I can't let you hurt her. And I don't care what I have to do to stop something from happening to her."

Mase scoffed out loud, jerking his chin forward. "You're the only risk to her. Not to mention yourself and the rest of us – just look at you."

Tsuki's eyes flared even darker. "Say that again!"

The human's brow raised at the cat's sharp tone, but before he could even open his mouth to spit out another remark, Tsuki snapped. Her eyes crackled with arcane anger, and in an instant she was flinging her hands forwards and releasing a deep burst of dark energy.

Although the burst missed the fire knight by a wide breath, it was enough to turn the already tense atmosphere in the room on its head in a single second – with Illusionary, Ika, and Mystic stepping back out of shock, and the queen half-standing up out of her throne.

Mase himself merely stepped forward, however – spreading out his arms, and summoning a powerful barrier of flame across his shirt and skin.

"So there it is. I always knew it."

Seeming increasingly worried, Mystic glanced over at them with urgency. "Why do you provoke her, Mase? She can't control this. Stand down now!" she yelled.

Mase shook his head and spat over his shoulder. "She knows what she's doing, Mystic. She wants this."

No sooner had he finished summoning his armor than Tsuki lunged forward with an angry cry – attempting to tackle him, and beating at his new defenses. But for now Mase remained entirely in control of the situation, tossing her off without appearing to exert much effort at all.

Landing with a heavy thud, Tsuki bucked about in a frantic scramble to recover her feet, and issued a sharp, feral hiss. Before she could fully come about to face him again, however, Mase blasted a brief line of flame in her direction, and she was forced to stagger back and repel it with a burst of her own magic – dispersing both effects with enough force to cause those watching on to stagger back some.

Ika, Mystic, and Yuuto were bristling more and more with every passing moment, but in contrast to them, and although he had retreated furthest away out of all others, Illusionary's face was… unreadable. Purely 'interested', if anything – even as Tsuki's fighting devolved further and further, and more and more of her form was consumed by the dark energy she was emanating and spewing in Mase's direction.

One particularly powerful deflecting cast from the fire knight caused one of the banners hanging from the walls of the throne room to sparkle with embers, and Tsuki to be shaken in her stance. But then, just before Mase could advance and lash out with his magic once more, the Queen stepped in from the side, raised her hands, and bowed her head.

"Halt."

Almost as though summoned by Upholder's voice alone, an enormous force rippled against Tsuki's form and properly pushed her off her feet – leaving her to land on her back and scramble in an attempt to right herself as Upholder moved to position herself between the cat and Mase.

Upholder sighed deeply and shook her head, arms slowly falling to her sides, but taking on a deep glow of radiant energy as they did so. "I'm giving you one more chance, Tsuki. Calm yourself. Control it. I don't want to do this."

Mase stepped a little back to where Ika and Mystic stood at this – not wanting to involve himself now that the queen's own authority and power was directly in play.

The cat woman finally recovered her footing and came to a low crouch with another hiss – darkness seeping off of all her limbs, and radiating in powerful waves from the pits of her eyes. There was an almost twisted nature to her, now – the angle of her joints feral and unnatural, and her fur singed and disheveled.

Kicking forward towards Upholder, she lunged at the queen – opening her maw, and snapping with clear intention to rip and tear.

The golden hound was far faster, however – moving with supernatural speed to give herself distance to defend and levelling her sword across her body to deflect the oncoming rush – but before the two could clash, Illusionary bowed his head from the sidelines, and raised a single palm in the direction of the fight. "Shine."

The blast that came next shot across the room and met Tsuki directly in the face – interjecting not with force, but with a burning, piercing bolt of light that lit the faces of all present and the tapestries on the walls a bright white.

Tsuki gave a rough, demonic-sounding hiss and raised one ragged, darkened arm to her face, but before she could reel back fully or regain her eyesight, the Queen moved forward, hefted her sword, and sent it striking forward with no hesitation.

The blow landed clean. Light pierced through dark, and before anyone else in the room could do more than gasp, the glistening tip of Upholder's sword emerged from Tsuki's black-stained back, before quickly withdrawing as the Queen stepped back into a ready fighting stance.

Mase exhaled hard through his helmet at the sight and allowed the last of his armor to fade to nothing – struck wordless. That he hadn't expected, no matter how much spite he had felt towards the feline woman, and how truthfully he had meant his antagonizing words.

For the longest, tensest moment, silence reigned, and the lifelessness of Tsuki's twisted, corrupted form became more and more apparent. The dark stopped emanating from her, her limbs went limp, and eventually, she slumped on her side to lay on motionless upon the ornate, clean stones of the throne room floor.

Stepping forward from the Queen's throne, Kijury first started at the darkened body that had once been Tsuki, and then towards Upholder. "You... didn't have to."

Taking a deep, steading breath, and allowing her own fiery energy to fade to its usual barely-noticeable but still present glow, the queen shook her head. "Look at her. I could sense it... consuming her. Even if I had have been able to neutralize her... I don't think there would have been much of Tsuki left. And I wasn't prepared to risk letting anyone else here die in hopes of finding out."

Mystic raised a hand to her mouth and turned away with a gasp and a tear in her eye, unable to bear looking upon Tsuki's body anymore. "She has a child."

"So she does." Now it was Ika's turn to shake her head. "Do you think she will become... like this, too?"

Kijury nodded, though his voice and form was still shaky. "From what we understand of magic, the chances are high she inherited these... powers. This curse."

"Then there is no question about it. We must do something, before the child develops such powers," Upholder declared, elegant muzzle held low, still stood above Tsuki's body. "We can't take the risk of this happening again."

"Please don't tell me we're killing a child..." Mase muttered, sighing.

The queen's face darkened. "No. We will avoid having to take... this kind of action again at any cost. She'll train to use her powers when she's older, and for now..."

She too sighed, looking over at her other knights. "We must clean up the mess Mase has brought to our door. Ika – see to a burial."

"And Yuuto, Mystic... please notify her husband as best, and as gently as you can."

Daku was above Harmony's crib when he heard the knock at the door. A few steps and moments later, and he was at the threshold opening it – allowing the patchy sunlight from the tree-lined village road outside to spill in about his feet.

First he saw Yuuto – sword sheathed at his waist, mask and horns impassive as ever – and then Mystic stood beside him with an expression on her soft human face that was far more readable, and far more foreboding.

"Mr. Mei." The masked man spoke with little infection. A long second passed, before he followed those words up with more.

"Tsuki is dead."

More silence. Mystic huffed with obvious anxiety.

"This has to be a joke," Daku finally said, letting out a breathless half-laugh.

Yuuto shook his impassive, mask-bearing head. "It couldn't be further from one. She lost her mind. Attacked Mase, and then the queen."

Face torn by bewilderment, Daku shook his head rapidly. "She said she was controlling-"

Mystic interrupted him with a pleading glance. "She's really gone, Daku."

That stunned him for a few seconds. And when the male cat did speak again, it was in a much more subdued, desperate tone. "Where is she? I want to see her."

"The body..." Now it was Yuuto's turn to shake his head. "Is not hers anymore. I'm not sure what it is or was, anymore."

It took the cat's demeanor and mind a long time to begin to visibly grapple with the weight of how serious the situation was – leaving the cat in a stunned silence as the two knights watched on.

"Was Tsuki acting differently since the birth, Daku?" Mystic asked.

Daku still didn't respond. The male cat simply stood still and silent, his eyes locked upon the stone pavers of the house's threshold.

The blue-haired woman's eyebrows raised in earnest exasperation. "She was, wasn't she? We... told you, Daku. That we'd need to know, if *anything* changed."

Something in the feline's frame broke, then. Tears began to make lines down his cheeks, and his breathing caught visibly within his chest. "I thought it would be f-fine..." He raised one hand to first wipe at the tears and then press hard against his muzzle. "She'd just given birth, for Ophin's sake. I just wanted to leave her in peace, let her return to service... she said she needed it. I just trusted her"

Watching the cat come apart with arms folded solemnly, Yuuto shook his head darkly and muttered. "And look where that got us."

Daku's crying turned to sobbing. "I can't tell Harmony about this... ever..."

Visibly holding herself back from taking a step forward to comfort him, Mystic shook her head. "Daku that's... that can't be your choice alone. From what we understand, it is almost certain that the child will have the same powers as her mother."

That made Daku growl and angrily run a paw across his face. "I cannot deny that my wife may have been in... may have been a danger. To herself and to others. That I erred greatly in becoming blinded and lazy, be it out of love. But my daughter..."

The male cat straightened his back and met both Yuuto and Mystic's eyes in turn in a forced, proud way. "I will not let the same happen to her. I know, now. And I will not fail again. Do not dare to question a father."

Yuuto opened his mouth with a rapid-fire response on his tongue, but the sound of footsteps on the path behind them came at this moment, and the three turned to see a robe-bearing, spotty-furred figure approaching from down the way. Illusionary, carrying a small wooden box in his hands.

"The convictions of a father." Drawing within speaking range, the cheetah gave a sardonic chuckle. "I do not question yours, Daku. Least of all in a... tragic moment like this. And I hope my faith is warranted, in that you recognize this situation as beyond your scope."

Yuuto greeted the priest's appearance with a short nod, holding his earlier conviction back for now. "I appreciate your haste in labor on such short notice, Illusionary."

The cheetah dismissed the gratitude with a wave of his hand. "You would be surprised by the passion I can summon in moments of need." He inclined his head in Daku's direction once more. "Where is your daughter?"

Daku bristled visibly. "You'll lay no hand on her."

Illusionary hesitated for a moment, before shrugging gently. "As you wish. It is unimportant." He took a few steps forward, and hefted the box in his hands towards the male cat. "Your daughter will remain in your care, so long as you accept our guidance insofar as the necessary precautions."

The other feline accepted the item reluctantly. "And this is?"

"Open it." The cheetah bowed his head expectantly. "It's for Harmony. To keep her safe."

Daku obeyed, although slowly and with tears still forming in the corners of his eyes. Inside lay a series of small, corked vials – each containing a black, viscous substance that appeared to glisten a little.

Concerned, he looked back up at Illusionary with an even deeper scowl. "You want me to drug my daughter?"

Mystic interjected before the priest could. "I feel you of all people should know the possible danger your daughter could face if she follows after her mother, Daku. Those will suppress her urges to release the darkness, and stop us from having to... take any action we don't want to."

Daku's eyes widened at that, seeming threatened by Mystic's words. "What in Ophin's name are you talking about?"

"If you need more, you know where to find me." Illusionary bowed his head again, turned about, and returned in the direction from which he had came.

Mystic ignored the priest's departure, and instead reached forward to put a hand on Daku's shoulder in a clear attempt to offer comfort. "Daku, just listen. None of us wanted this. The queen didn't want this. Please..."

But Daku pushed her hand off, and turned to face away into the doorway of his house. "Don't touch me. Not after what you've done – all of you. Just go."

Yuuto let out a tired sigh at this, and obeyed Daku's command – turning about, and beginning to make his way back down the village path as well at no particular rush. Mystic lingered for a little longer, watching with tears in the corners of her eyes as Daku stormed back into his house with the sound of muffled sobs, but followed in turn as the door slammed before her.

Daku's steps were slow, drained, and numb as he tracked through the lounge, and back into the bedroom Harmony's crib stood in the corner. Seeing his child wrapped in her soft cloths, looking up at him with those completely oblivious, innocent eyes, almost made him burst out into sobs once more. But he couldn't bear to let her see. *She may have lost her mother... but I will stay strong for her. No matter what. Even if I don't trust Illusionary, don't trust the knights... I can't take the risk of losing you too.*

Moving slowly and with great weight in his heart, Daku placed the box down on the dresser next to the crib, and slowly opened it. Taking one vial out with shaky hands, he held it up, clasped the stopper, and pulled it free.

A few steps and he was above Harmony's crib, looking down on her as she stared back up with her innocent, wide eyes. Another moment and he was lowering the vial to her lips – cradling her back and head to help her sip a few drops of the medicine down.

No sooner did he consider himself finished than Harmony gave a little burp, tossed her head, and closed her eyes. "Someone's tired." Daku closed the vial and laid it back in its box before carefully raising his daughter out of her crib and cradling her in his arms while she began to snore quietly.

"We'll get through this, my precious daughter," he whispered.

2

*T*en years later

It's calling for you, Harmony. Let it take you in. Let it cradle you. Let it take care of you. It is you. It knows everything you want – everything you've ever wanted, in the dark corners of your mind. If you just let it, it could-

"No!"

The word ripped from her mouth unconsciously, before she could even so much as feel her body or thoughts. Once it had, however, her ears registered the cry's echo throughout her room, and the fear running through her brain reached the rest of her body.

The young cat shot up in bed with a shiver – hyperventilating, and eyes wide. Yet, as she urgently glanced about at the morning light-cast walls of her bedroom, she saw nothing but her closet, desk, and the mess of toys scattered around the floor.

It took a long few seconds for Harmony to collect herself and shake off the 'bad dream', despite the fact that it wasn't exactly anything new to her, but eventually she stretched out her arms and climbed over the side of her small wooden bed.

Letting out a sigh, she stood, and raised her head up to the black, painted-star bespeckled ceiling above her to stretch her neck. *Another nightmare, another day... Without school, without friends.*

Her nose twitched in the air. *But at least it smells like there's breakfast.*

"Harmony? Are you up? Make sure you clean up your room before coming down for breakfast, and don't forget to take your medicine!" A voice called from down the hall. Her father's.

"Yes, Dad!" She meowed out in response, interrupting her stretch to direct her voice to the doorway. *I don't want to clean, I'm too hungry... but I also don't want Dad to be mad.*

Stooping down hastily, she plucked up a few toys – a wooden toy train, a short-limbed cloth doll – and placed them into her painted toy organizer, before brushing aside a few more items with her feet and scrambling up to leave the room. She was almost out and in the hallway before her thoughts caught up with her, and she whipped back around to her desk, where a small wooden box filled with small black vials stool open. *My medicine.*

Stepping over to the desk and plucking up one of the vials, Harmony moved her hand to its cork. Before she could unfasten it, however, a voice echoed in her head – her own thoughts, or the one from her dreams? She couldn't quite be sure. *You don't need it. You never did.*

Blinking in shock, she stared down at the vial in confusion for a few seconds. "I... don't?" she whispered out loud.

A few seconds passed, but the voice did not return. Yet although it seemed to have faded, the girl's confusion had not. She remained staring at the vial, before slowly, gradually placing it down into the box with the others.

Feeling only a little hesitant, she then turned about and began to pace out of her room. *Maybe I don't need it after all. Dad never told me why I need it. And it does get so boring to have to remember.*

Turning about the hall, Harmony made her way into the kitchen to see her Dad dressed in plain clothes and a black apron, tending to the stove. His back was turned to her, his tail swaying slightly, and his hand moving a pan.

She skipped over to stand by his side, and glanced around his form at what was inside the pan. *Bacon!* "Morning, Dad!"

"Good morning, my precious daughter!" he answered, switching hands on the pan to give her a light stroke on the head.

Purring, the cat girl watched him cook. "Did you make..."

"Pancakes?" Daku cut her off and revealed a plate of golden pancakes next to him on the counter with a chuckle. "I know my daughter well!"

"I can't wait to eat!" Smiling enthusiastically, Harmony made over to the table and hopped into her chair.

Her father chuckled as he shuffled the pan. "Someone's energetic today! Did you drink your medicine?"

Don't tell him!

Mid-settling into her seat, Harmony froze up as the voice echoed through her head, before slowly shifting down the rest of the way. "O-of course, Dad!"

Daku smiled, turning back to the bacon. "Good!"

Harmony hung her head as she waited for food. *Dad will be really mad at me if he finds out that I didn't drink my medicine... but I shouldn't worry.*

But then there was a light clatter, and the heavy scent of bacon filled her nose. She glanced up, and saw a full plate in front of her on the table.

"Food!" she mewed happily, her tail swaying.

Sitting down, he set his plate on the table. "Well, dig in!"

Wasting little time, she picked up her utensils and began to eat ferociously. Daku's eyes widened as he watched his daughter eat like a feral beast.

She stopped eating for a second, looking over at her father's expression. "What?" she meowed through a mawful of food.

"Nothing. Just didn't think you were so hungry!" Daku gave a chuckle.

The cat girl smiled and swallowed before continuing to eat – leaving her father to dig in as well, and the two to sit together in silence for a while.

Harmony was very glad that they had time together like this, now that her father didn't have to go to work. He had persisted with his business for a few years, which she could barely remember, but now he didn't have to leave anymore. She didn't know where he got the house's gold from, but she believed it had something to do with the Kingdom.

After she was finished, Harmony was quick to hop up from the table, wash her hands at the sink, and dart over towards the kitchen doorway. "I'm going to play outside, Dad!"

Still yet to finish his own meal, Daku glanced over and nodded – though by the time he did so, his daughter was already out in the lounge and making over to the front door. "Okay, but be careful, sweetie."

"I will!" She called back, hand on the latch.

Yet, though she remembered stepping out into the brightness of the day, and although she remembered the smell of the trees and the cobblestones beneath her feet... she didn't remember going out into the yard, and she didn't remember feeling or doing anything past that point.

Before long, in fact, she didn't remember much at all.

Chirping birds, creaking wood, and rushing waters echoed throughout Penlight Forest. And amidst them – a single set of booted footsteps.

A masked figure walked amidst the trees – a skinny sword sheathed on their waist, and a brown hood over their crooked horns. Their pace did not continue for long, however, before a dash of slick red upon the ground caught their eye, and they soon knelt to investigate.

"An animal couldn't have made this mark..." they murmured to themselves. A quick glance upwards identified that the streak ran between a few trees to the side of the path, and a few steps forward in that direction led to a scene of... incomprehensible gory horror.

The corpse was a bear. Or, at least, it had used to be a bear. A mix of amazement and horror filled them as the figure examined the corpse closer – with no claw marks to note, it was almost as though the beast had been beaten and torn apart with... sheer might alone.

The masked figure raised their head, and sighed darkly.

Something's not right. Not right at all.

"Hi? Hello there! Are you okay?"

Harmony gasped as though it were the first breath she'd taken in minutes – sitting up with a start just as she had that morning. Only this time, everything was different. She wasn't in her room, for one, and right in front of her was the inquisitive, concerned face of a young, bipedal red dragon.

That was enough to ground her in confusion, as she struggled to comprehend everything going on. *A red... dragon?* She'd heard of their kind among some of the other rarer species of folk that inhabited the kingdom, but she'd never seen one before.

At second glance, the girl appeared to be about the same age as she herself was, had golden eyes, and bore a wide smile as she sat down next to where Harmony was laying on the ground. "What are you doing out here all alone?"

Sitting up and breathing hard through her disorientation, Harmony looked about at her surroundings to see that she was sat next to a clear, glistening pond, and surrounded by tall, noble trees. *A... forest? The Penlight forest?*

"Did you hurt yourself?" the dragon inquired again, though Harmony had yet to answer her earlier questions.

"W-What are you talking about...?" Harmony replied, her voice shaking.

The dragon pointed towards the cat girl's paws. "You're bleeding!"

Harmony looked down, and her eyes widened. Her fingers, pads, and claws were stained with a scarlet substance that she could only assume was blood.

"N-No... no!" The cat panicked, quickly turning about and dipping paws in the water flowing next to her, scrubbing her paws as hard as she could to get the blood off.

The dragon tilted her head to the side, and reached one paw out to touch Harmony's shoulder. "What happened?"

Harmony recoiled drastically – pulling back and instead rubbing harder at her paws. "Don't touch me!"

But then something caught her attention in the clear waters she was washing herself in, and her heart stopped. Looking at her reflection in the pond, she found her eyes were pitch black.

Screaming out loud and scrambling back away from the pond, she almost lost her footing completely in her surprise. The dragon seemed only confused. "What's wrong? Do your grabbers still hurt?" she questioned.

"Why were my eyes like that!" the cat yelled, distressed.

The dragon shrugged, seeming just a little taken aback. "I dunno!"

Breathing heavily, she tried to process what she'd seen in her reflection. *That wasn't me! That wasn't me!* The thoughts sped through her mind.

"I'm Irin Ishii!" the dragon greeted her, right back to smiling. "What's your name?"

"Harmony Mei... I live in the village... near here?"

The dragon girl smiled. "That's so cool! I live near the castle, with my Mom and Dad."

"You live near the castle?" That brought great joy and surprise to Harmony's face. "I've always wanted to go there, but my Dad never takes me..."

Tail swaying and head tilted to the side, Irin's curiosity was openly apparent. "Did you ever ask your Mom?"

Harmony shook her head. "I don't know my Mom."

Irin's eyes widened earnestly. "You don't?! That must be sad. But at least we can be friends?"

Smiling back, Harmony nodded. "Great, let's..."

But then she stopped – feeling as though her tongue had been held still against its will. Those words, this feeling... triggered something within her. A great happiness, but also a great possessiveness, and even a little... anger.

The dragon girl's curiosity quickly turned to confusion as Harmony groaned, and slowly began to hunch down at the waist. "W-what's wrong? Is it your paws, do they hurt?"

But Harmony ignored her – instead raising her head and her right paw to point behind her new friend. A masked, cloaked figure was slowly, cautiously moving through the trees towards them.

"Oh! That's Yuuto! He's a knight from the kingdom." the dragon turned about to wave. "Hi, Yuuto!"

Moving a little faster now, the knight approached the two – stance still wary, and hand lightly on the hilted sword by his side.

The nearer the masked man drew, the more Harmony could feel energy welling up within her arms, chest, and body – flooding up into her brain, and into the paws which she had washed of blood just seconds ago.

The knight bowed his head. "Harmony, calm yourself. I'm not here to hurt you."

At first she blinked. *How does he know my name?* But then the dark feelings flared much, much hotter. *He wants to take your new friend away! You can't let him.*

Surrounding her paw in dark energy, she spat back at the small dragon to her side. "Stay behind me, Irin!"

"But that's just Yuuto..."

Harmony cut the dragon off. "I won't let him take you from me!"

Now stood just mere feet away, Yuuto sighed. "I didn't think I'd have to use this..." The horned, masked man took his sword out of its sheath.

Irin gasped. "Don't hurt her, please!"

But the knight didn't move to strike with his sword – instead closing his eyes, speaking under his breath, and issuing a sharp jolt of arcane energy that struck the cat girl just as she was beginning to hiss under her breath and preparing to pounce.

Soon, her gaze become unfocused, her body limp, and she crumbled to the floor – energy fading, and young, small body looking incredibly fragile.

Irin's eyes widened and shot back towards Yuuto in fear. "What did you do to her?"

"Nothing harmful," Yuuto answered, sheathing his sword. "Just something to... give us enough time to figure out what's happening here."

"Harmony..."

Who's there? She thought, distantly recognizing that she was laying on something soft with her eyes closed.

"Harmony!"

Her eyes shot open for the third time that day, and when they did, she saw her father looking down back at her. Now she *was* in her bedroom, her sheets around her, and evening light filtering through the window.

The only thing out of place was the knight that had approached earlier – Yuuto, Irin had called him – standing in the center of the room, and watching her with his mask as unreadable as before.

Not paying the other man any mind, however, she threw herself towards her father and immediately drew him into a hug. "Dad! I didn't drink my medicine... I'm sorry, I'm sorry!" she cried into his shoulder.

"Calm down, Harmony," Daku reassured, patting his daughter's back. "It's fine... Yuuto told me what happened."

She continued to sob for a moment, but shortly after there was a yawn from off to the side, and her head jerked over to see a familiar red dragon girl sitting up from the small chair in the corner with her arms outstretched. "Urgh... Is Harmony awake yet?"

Breaking out of the hug with her father, Harmony sat up out of bed, ran over to her new friend, and wrapped her up in a tight embrace instead. "Irin! I didn't hurt you!"

"Harmony!" Irin leant into the hug and smiled. "I'm super happy you're okay too."

Yuuto looked back at Daku while the two remained close. "I'll have to tell Upholder about this. You know that, right?"

At first Daku stiffened visibly at this, but then he turned to his daughter with a forced smile. "Harmony – you and your new friend can go play in your room, okay?"

The girl reacted almost immediately, reaching out to grab Irin's arm enthusiastically and taking them both to stand. "Alright! Come on, Irin."

Giving a little giggle, Irin allowed herself to be led out of the room – leaving Yuuto and Daku alone as the two girls' chattering faded between the walls.

The moment they were gone for good, the male cat growled and rubbed at his head. "You know my feelings on this, after what you did to my wife. You know that this is my responsibility. Why can you not keep your hands on out my fur?"

"I can't let this go by, Daku." The masked man shook his head. "The queen and the knights will come here eventually. Harmony's powers are dangerous, and she's only a child."

Daku heaved an enormous sigh. "And I have no power in this situation, it would seem. But you can at least leave me in peace with my defeat."

For a long, silent moment, Yuuto's impassive mask stared back at Daku, before he bowed his head, folded his hands, and steppe back towards the door behind him. "As you wish."

Daku neglected to watch as he opened the door and moved through, but some time after the knight's departure, he lifted his head and looked towards Harmony's room, hearing the two girls' voices chirping on, and their laughter echoing through the halls.

At least Harmony has a friend now...

The throne room had been quiet except for occasional whispering for quite some time when Yuuto's rushed footsteps began to echo through it. Upholder's ears perked from where she sat at the noise, bringing her to lean forward in her throne and remove her thin knuckles from the bridge of her muzzle. Kijury moved somewhat back from her side, and Ika and Mystic stood to either side of them at attention bristled somewhat at the noise too.

When the masked man finally came into vision, it was at a heightened pace – so much so that the Queen raised a hand to hail him down before he could come much closer. "Greetings, Yuuto. You seem ill at ease. What happened on your patrol?"

He reached the center of the hall before coming to a sharp halt, and bowing his head. "I have a report to deliver, my queen. The child... Harmony..."

The queen sat up in her throne in clear panic at this, but Yuuto quickly raised both hands to reassure her. "She is well. Daku has her back under control. Only... she was wild, for a moment. I know not how long, but it would appear that she didn't take Illusionary's medicine."

Upholder's golden hair flared flamelike for a moment. "Was anybody hurt?

Yuuto shook his head. "Not any person, at least that I know of. But in the forest... who knows what damage she did."

That seemed to placate the queen a little, as she settled back in her throne, but continued to watch tensely as Yuuto paced a little and continued to speak. "I found her in the company of another girl. Irin Ishi. Docile at first, and seemingly disorientated. But then the energy began to surge again, and I was forced to step in."

He came to a hard stop, and met the queen's eyes once more with deep sincerity. "I'm not sure what would have happened, had I not have been there. The dragon girl seemed able to defend herself, but she too is... naïve, and lacks control."

"What, does she have powers too?"

Yuuto looked over to see the human fire knight Mase Yaketsuku emerging from a side passage along the wall to the right of Upholder's throne – dressed in his usual white shirt and black trousers, and bearing his usual cynical scowl. "Nothing we need more than another dangerous brat to deal with."

"From what she showed me, she appears to possess some type of stone magic. Most likely also hereditary." The forest knight bowed his head, trying to keep his cool in the face of Mase's abrasiveness. "I recommend that, when the time comes, we train her as well. It could make things smoother for Harmony to have someone here that she knows."

Mystic looked to Upholder at this. "What do you think, my Queen?"

The hound looked to the foot of her throne for a long moment, thinking deeply before issuing an answer. "We will wait. For a while longer."

Mase's eyebrows raised at this. "How long is a while longer? How long can we afford? I warned against Tsuki, and I was correct. So I warn again now. We should take action immediately."

"He has a point." Ika added. "How are we to know if Harmony is losing control of her powers – like Tsuki did – before it's too late?"

Glaring at Mase in response to his borderline insubordinate tone, Upholder spoke up. "I won't let that happen. Not this time. This time we know the risks all too well. She has Illusionary's medicine, and where we failed Tsuki, I..."

She lowered her head and flowing hair with a deep sigh. "We will ensure to not fail Harmony."

Mase's pale-skinned face remained rigid all throughout the queen's speech, and even after she finished, brash thoughts could still be seen flashing behind his eyes. For a long moment it seemed inevitable that the fire knight would open his lips and spit them out, but then he too breathed deeply, and averted his eyes from all others in the room. "I heed your word, milady. Though my warning remains firm."

With that, the fire knight turned sharply on his heel and began to stride away through the hall at a stern pace, leaving Ika, Kijury, Mystic, and the queen watching after with dire expressions. Illusionary, however, remained still with his hands politely folded – waiting for the queen to acknowledge his presence once more.

Upholder sighed and bowed her head again at the sound of Mase's footsteps echoing further and further away – sinking back into her throne as Ika and Mystic traded nervous, uncertain glances.

They knew better than to question the queen's competence and power, but they had seen – felt – Tsuki's power all those years ago, and thus couldn't help but hear Mase's words echoing through their heads. What good could come, in truth, from standing by and allowing that danger to grow?

But what other choice did they have?

3

Five years later

   No... no... please, no more... Just let me go...

It was happening again. As it did increasingly often, these nights. On the outside, nestled amongst the spread-out mess of her discarded sheets, Harmony was tossing and turning, but on the inside, she was clawing at the walls of her prison – the suffocating, impenetrable dark keeping her trapped inside herself and inside terrible, terrible dreams.

Finally, the storm broke. Jolting awake with a sharp gasp for air, Harmony shot up in bed, and glanced around urgently. Yet, as usual, she was greeted with nothing more than her moonlight-cast bedroom.

Tears prickled in her eyes. Desperate to get away from her earlier paralysis and the source of the voices, Harmony swung her legs over the edge of the bed, and blundered through the darkened room towards her table where her medicine box stood. She had taken a sip last night, she... swore, or hadn't she?

Reaching down with a small, shaking hand, she took up one vial. But as soon as she had done so, a voice screamed in her head. *No!*

"W-Who are you? Please... this time, answer me." Her speech shook, battling with the voice within her ears.

Do not take that poison. The voice ignored Harmony's question. *Destroy it now – or you will regret it.*

Staring down at the vial, she whispered. "Why? I don't... understand."

Though she waited ten long seconds or more, the voice didn't respond, and soon a spike of anger flared up within her. "Answer me!"

Destroy it! The voice boomed in her head. *Do it now. Now!*

Harmony, and threw the bottle of medicine to shatter upon her table. "Get them to stop! Get them to stop!"

"Harmony?" First her father's voice was distant, and then the sound of rapid footsteps approached, until Daku was standing in her doorway with his sleep clothes on and a worried look in his eyes.

"What happened?" Still moving urgently, Daku moved over to her and wrapped his daughter in a tight hug.

"The voices..." she began. "I want them to stop... They won't answer me!"

Daku tightened his hug. "That's what the medicine is for, Harmony. If you keep up your schedule, drink it regularly... things will get better, I promise."

Harmony wanted to believe him. His words made sense – they were the ones she'd heard her entire life, and that had long since faded into daily routine. But they like claws against her brain, now – the voices screamed against her father's reason, and darkness welled up within her with a strength like nothing she'd felt before.

Suddenly, all other sensation faded, and for a brief, blinding moment, she felt everything that had been locked up inside exploding outwards – losing all sense in the static, all-consuming noise for a second, until it faded, and all was quiet.

Still shaking, and even more bewildered than before, Harmony tried to squeeze into her father's hug harder, but... he was gone. Her eyes blinked open, first glancing forward, then left, then right, and then... down.

That when she saw him – just in front of her. Daku lay motionless on the floor, blood leaking from wounds along his chest, and his maw. His eyes were soulless. *No... no!*

She collapsed down and began to shake her father's body. "Wake up, Dad! Please!" Tears upon endless tears ran down her face as she shook her Dad's stiff form.

This is your fault, Harmony. You killed him. He's dead because of you!

"N-No! I did nothing!" she yelled back, though knowing all too well how foolish her words sounded. How futile her denial was.

Legs buckling, and arms slowly failing to allow her father's form to slip to the floor, Harmony closed her eyes as hard as she could. Everything felt like it was crushing in around her – the air, her skull, her eyes. "Stop! Get out of my head!"

But they didn't stop. The voices in her head got louder, louder, and louder – until she could only scream at the top of her lungs to drown them out. She screamed on and on, and the room was filled with darkness – darkness that never ended.

No longer just inside her. But strong, and deeply, deeply hungry.

"Dad!"

Harmony stood in her father's doorway – panting, crying, and dressed in her plain cloth pajamas.

Daku sat up almost instantly at his daughter's cry – jumping out of bed, and moving towards her with open arms. "What's wrong, Harmony? What happened?"

Hurriedly, the girl ran over to her father, hugging him. Tears stained his shirt as he embraced the hug and stroked the back of her daughter's head. "Calm down, Harmony..." he comforted her. "Talk to me and tell me what happened."

She shook in his arms. "I had a... scary dream. The voices, they..."

Daku stroked her head as she struggled to speak. "Don't worry, Harmony. It was just a nightmare. And the voices... won't bother you in your dreams, so long as you make sure to drink your medicine."

Sniffling, she pressed her face into her father's stomach. "Will it really make them go away?" she questioned.

He broke out of the hug, his paws now on her shoulders. "They will, my precious daughter," he answered, kissing her forehead before wiping the tears from her eyes. "But for now, I should thank you for waking me up. Might not haven gotten everything ready in time if you hadn't."

He chuckled and tightened his embrace a little. "Most importantly, happy sixteenth birthday, my precious daughter."

Harmony's eyes widened in surprise, fear completely forgotten – the significance of the day and the morning had completely slipped her brain. Her tail even began to sway in happiness. "Thanks, Dad!"

He purred in sync with her for a moment before breaking the hug. "Irin and her parents over will be here before long, so I'll be in the kitchen. Just make sure you drink your medicine, okay?"

Harmony rolled her eyes. "I will, don't worry, Dad."

Smiling, her father left the room and headed over to the kitchen. Harmony sighed, walking over to her room, where the wooden box sat upon her desk, and picked up one of the vials within it.

I've been drinking this for as long as I can remember... Harmony thought, examining the liquid within. *And yet I still have no idea what it does.*

Harmony opened the bottle and gave it a whiff. It didn't smell like anything. *Maybe, just to see...*

She corked the bottle, and put it back in the box.

A few steps later, she was back out in the hall and glancing about the threshold of the kitchen to see her father facing the table with his apron on. She giggled out of excitement. *He must be working on the cake! He was up so late last night preparing it.*

"No peeking! You'll have to wait until it's ready!" Daku called.

Harmony rolled her eyes, but smiled. "Fine! Want me to wait in the living room?"

He nodded, and she nearly turned to leave, but glanced back over her shoulder just before moving back through the threshold. "Have you..."

"They'll be here soon." He answered, still working away at cooking.

Nodding, she skipped out of the kitchen and to the living room, where she sat on the couch and let her tail sway. *I can't wait to see them.*

But then her thoughts wandered a little, and her smile turned to a frown. *If it wasn't for what happened that day, in the forest... I wouldn't have met her. My eyes that day... how did I do that?*

Harmony looked down at her right paw – making a fist, and concentrating as hard as she could.

The cat girl focused hard, as though the answers to her countless questions were held somewhere in her grasp. *Dad can't, nobody else in the village can. It's almost as if-*

Knock. Knock. Knock.

Her head shot towards the front door with a gasp, the black aura fading from her paw as she hopped up and ran over to it to hastily hinge the door open. *Irin's here!*

No sooner had she done so, however, and before she could speak, than she was wrapped up into darkness, and a sudden loss of air cut her off. "Happy Birthday, Harmony!" a male voice spoke from above, rumbling against her front.

"Th-thanks! But can you please stop killing me while you hug me, Mr. Ishii?" She struggled to get out.

"Oh. Oops! My apologies, Harmony!" The bulky, rough-dressed male dragon stepped back with a wide grin.

Harmony smiled. "Don't worry, Mr. Ishii. Are Mrs. Ishii and Irin here?"

"You bet! Hi there, Harmony!" An older female red dragon peeked over Mr. Ishii's left shoulder, barely visible behind his height.

The cat girl opened her mouth to greet Dorthro's wife, but before she could, a brighter, younger response rang through the air, and she glanced over to the side to spot a flurry of movement and the appearance of her best friend.

Harmony's smile widened, and she spread her arms wide. "Irin!"

Irin slipped past her father and brought the cat into a tight hug. "Harmony!"

The two best friends embraced each other for some time, giggling all the while, before a voice from behind them inside the house caused them to shift about. "Glad to see you all here!"

All four standing in the doorway turned about to see Daku in the threshold of the kitchen – apron still on, and a rare true smile on his face.

"Hey, Mr. Mei!" Irin replied.

Shifting past Harmony and his daughter into the house with an awkward shuffle, Dorthro walked over to Daku and wrapped his arms around the white-furred cat as well. "Good to see you, Daku!"

"Good to see you too, Dorthro!" Daku managed to choke out against the tight, constricting embrace.

"Let him breathe, Dorthroruth" Mrs. Ishii told her husband – stepping past as well and administering a reprimanding tone.

"Right, right." Dorthro let go and nervously rubbed at the back of his neck. "My apologies, Daku!"

The cat man gave a stifled cough, before smiling and shaking his head. "Nothing to apologize for."

"It's nice to see you, Daku. And happy birthday to Harmony, of course!" The older female dragon walked over to the cat girl and wrapped her up in a tight hug.

Daku smiled. "It's nice to see you too, Anahita."

Anahita broke out of the hug with Harmony and glanced over to her father. "Do you need help with anything?"

"Cake needs finishing up, if you insist on lending a hand." Daku glanced over in the direction of the kitchen.

The male dragon's smile beamed even wider. "Let's get to work, then!"

Daku nodded gladly, and he and the two married dragons shuffled off into the kitchen, leaving Harmony and Irin standing in the entryway.

Harmony turned to her friend. "Wanna hang out in my room?"

Nodding, Irin gave a wide grin just like her father's. "Yeah!"

A few seconds later and they were both sat upon Harmony's bed – giggling, and watching the sun and birds through the window.

"So how does it feel to be sixteen now?" Irin asked with a light chuckle.

"It feels the same as when I was fifteen!" Harmony tilted her head, thinking the feeling and concept over.

The dragon girl kicked her legs back and forth off the edge of the bed. "I can't wait until we're older, though! We'll get to do so many things... like exploring places on our own, and being able to stay up as long as we want!"

Harmony nodded in agreement. "Yeah! Maybe we can get better using and learn about our abilities, too!"

Irin smiled. "Maybe! Have you talked to your Dad about them?"

The cat girl shook her head, face falling. "No. Anytime I ask, he avoids the question and does something else. It's annoying."

"Well, you can always..."

The voice from the kitchen cut Irin off. "Harmony! Come in here!"

Harmony's frown became a wide smile, and she hopped up. "Cake time!"

The two girls rushed out of the bedroom and into the living room, then the kitchen. When they entered, they were greeted by all three of their parents standing on the opposite end of the table, and a large, circular, chocolate-colored cake upon it.

"Happy birthday!" they all shouted in unison.

Harmony purred and ran over to her father, hugging him tightly. "Thanks, guys!"

The five of them sat down, next, except for Daku. "Now," He started, picking up the knife set to the side of the cake and then lowering it down to start cutting slices. "Let's have some cake!"

However, before they could truly start eating, there came a sharp rapping noise from the next room, and the heads of all present turned towards it.

Knock! Knock! Knock!

Daku sighed. "I'll get that." Placing the knife back down, he walked out of the kitchen and over to the door.

The Ishii family and Harmony stood alert and listening as light flooded into the lounge from the door being opened, and Daku's voice rose in agitation. "What are you doing here? You know that you aren't welcome."

A smooth, calm voice replied. "I am aware. I come only to congratulate her, and to speak over some important business."

There was some more flustered speech from Daku, and hushed returns from the second voice, but before long the cat sighed again and stepped back into the kitchen – this time followed by a tall, slim deer dressed in rough-spun but fine ropes, and carrying a long wooden staff with a carved head. "This is... an acquaintance of mine. Kijury Weathers."

The deer bowed towards Harmony, expression composed and neutral. "It is an honor to finally meet you, madam."

Harmony's eyes widened as the deer continued. "I am the personal guard of Upholder of the Penlight Kingdom."

Now her mouth fell straight open. "The queen!" She knew little of the kingdom and its knights, but that name she recognized.

Kijury nodded. "Indeed."

The deer made to continue, but Daku was quicker – raising his hand abruptly. "Enough. I believe it's time for you to leave."

Silence gripped the table. None of the three dragons sat about it so much as moved, let alone said a word, as incredibly uncharacteristic as this was for them.

Even Kijury seemed to stall for a moment before speaking once more – though much more carefully. "I wish for peace. I do not come here without knowledge of how... difficult it is for you." He bowed his head. "But the time has come for Harmony to hear what she always had to hear at some point. And you should grant her that much autonomy, Daku."

Although she was confused to say the least, hearing her name mentioned in such a curious manner was more than enough to drive Harmony to glance over to her father with pleading eyes. "Please, Dad. I want to hear what he has to say."

Daku locked tense gazes with her for a moment, but then let out a sigh and glanced over to Dorthro and his wife at either side of the table. "Fine. But let us have this conversation somewhere else."

Kijury bowed his head. "My apologies, I do understand that this is..."

But then he trailed off as Daku walked unceremoniously through the threshold leading to the lounge, before stepping after with Harmony in tow.

A few seconds later and Daku had himself seated on the couch, with Harmony springing up next to him. The deer remained standing, however, and folded his hands in front of his chest as he visibly composed himself to speak again.

"I want to talk about Harmony's powers."

Harmony blinked and glanced over as she felt her father tangibly stiffen on the seat next to her. *Powers, what does he mean?*

Yet Daku said nothing for now, and Kijury continued with a solemn expression. "In truth, I come on the queen's express orders. Your medicine has been keeping things in order, but in time, that will not be enough."

She could only blink over at her father in search of clarity. "What does he mean? My medicine, I don't..."

But Daku didn't acknowledge her – instead gesturing exasperatedly with one hand, and gripping at the edge of the couch with his other. "It's been... years since anything went wrong. I said it back then, and I will say it now – I demand respect and trust from the Queen in keeping my own daughter safe. That much you must afford me."

Kijury's face lost some of its politeness, and took on some determination. "There are greater responsibilities and stakes at play here than your stubbornness can be allowed to hinder, Daku. You know that. This is the time to act in the interest of safety, before it's too late." He took a step back in the direction of the front door, and bade Harmony a nod. "I will return tomorrow, madam. Your answer then will decide things."

Harmony nodded back at him, standing up from the couch. "O-okay, thanks!"

The deer smiled back at her, and turned about to properly make over to the door. His hand unfastened the latch, but before shifting into the sunlight beyond, he glanced over his shoulder once more. "And happy birthday, Harmony."

Then he was gone, and Harmony was vanishing back into the kitchen to rejoin the Ishii family. Staring at the door, Daku couldn't process what he just heard and witnessed and heard. The white-furred cat remained on the couch for a moment, putting his paws on his head. "I hate Upholder so fucking much..."

Eventually Daku joined his daughter and her dragon friends back in the kitchen, where the atmosphere before Kijury's visit had recovered somewhat. Eventually, after finishing her slice and placing her fork down, Harmony's face scrunched itself up, and she broke the awkward silence with a sharp glance towards her father. "I want to say yes, Dad."

Still to eat even half of his own portion, Daku shook his head darkly at the suggestion. "No. And I don't want to hear another word about it."

Harmony bristled but didn't push further – sitting with her arms crossed until the others had finished their slices of cake as well.

Dorthro wasn't one to let the silence linger, however, and cleared his throat loud enough that all present looked over as he grinned widely over at Harmony and his daughter. "You girls should take some coin and spend some time together near the castle. As your gift from us."

Irin's jaw dropped at this, and she watched with increasingly wide eyes as her father reached to his side and pulled out a number of small coins to place in her palm. "Can we really?"

Harmony was just as enthused. "Woah, uhm, sure. Sounds amazing!" She turned nervously to her father. "Dad?"

Daku exhaled, but eventually nodded. "Alright. After that visit, I think it would be nice. But be safe."

Harmony beamed back. "We will!"

Not wasting a single moment further, she turned tail to follow as Irin darted through the front door, leaving her father, Dorthro, and Anahita sitting about the table in silence for a long, long few minutes after they'd left.

It wasn't long before the girls' wandering took them to where they could see taller, more urban stone buildings in the distance, and Harmony was nearly squealing in excitement as they drew nearer and nearer. *This is going to be great!* Thought the cat.

Or a disaster.

Harmony gasped – stopping in her tracks and looking around, causing Irin to turn to her friend with a worried look. "What's wrong, Harmony?"

"N-Nothing! Let's keep going!" Her meow shook.

The dragon girl continued with a smile, and before they knew it, they were no longer standing before the castle's skyline but amongst it – through the gate, past the walls, and swallowed up amongst a fluctuating, busy mass of people of all species, ages, and appearances.

"Wow..." Harmony murmured under her breath in awe, neck craned back to look up at the banners and brightly painted facades all around her.

"I know, right? This place is enormous!" The red dragon giggled, leading her friend about a corner and into an even more packed street than the last.

Eventually, they came to the biggest store yet, out of all those they had seen already – a larger, squarish store with barrels and crates out front of it with a sign designating it as *Penlight Petty Trade* above the door.

Harmony pointed over to it enthusiastically. "Let's go in there!"

Nodding, Irin grabbed Harmony's paw and walked over. "Sure! The storekeeper knows my dad!"

With a jingle of the doorbell, they were inside and gazing eagerly about at the varied, messy contents of the shop. Before they proceeded deeper in, however, they came to the shop's counter, where a lean snake man stood with his arms leant forward on the wood in front of him. His scales and eyes were a dark purple color.

Irin beamed up at him. "Hi, Mr. Exousia!"

The snake man chuckled. "I told you to call me Archer, Irin! But who's this here?" He questioned, looking over at Harmony now.

"This is my best friend, Harmony Mei!" The dragon's tail wagged.

Harmony smiled. "Hi!"

But then Irin was tugging on Harmony's paw, already moving towards the store shelves. "Let's split up and look around!"

"Okay!" The cat girl bade the snake one last wave, before moving off alone through the store while glancing about curiously. So many shelves, so many items that she couldn't even begin to imagine functions for.

It's all so nice, isn't it? It could be yours, you know. The voice echoed in Harmony's head.

She stopped in her tracks. *What do you mean?*

Urgently, she glanced about for Irin. But she couldn't find the dragon girl – and instead, her eyes caught upon a palm-sized metal skull sat upon the upmost shelf in front of her. *That looks cool.*

Then take it.

Harmony's eyes widened. "W-What?" she whispered to herself.

No response in words came, but instead energy and compulsion began to take hold – welling up within her, moving her arms upwards of their own accord, and her paws towards the metal skull even as they shook.

She could feel the coolness of the object, and could feel distress wracking her brain, but she could not stop herself as her arms lowered down again, and pulled the item towards the folds of her clothes.

"Miss?"

Almost literally jumping where she stood, Harmony glanced up to her side to see the store owner Archer standing next to her. His face was confused, rather than angry or accusative, but the voices surged through her mind anyway – banging on the walls of her brain even harder than before. *He saw! End him, before it's too late.*

"N-no... Stop..." Harmony begged under her breath, unable to look the snake in the eyes.

"It's alright. You can..." The snake began charitably, arm reaching out, but then he frowned at the cat's distressed speech, and the visible energy covering her arms. "What's..."

Harmony's feet wobbled, her body pulsed with energy, and her eyes unfocussed – no longer able to see Archer, no longer after to speak, and no longer able to stop the voices inside from yelling louder, louder, and louder, until –

It all exploded outwards – all the force, and all the turmoil. Harmony felt it leaving her form, heard a great crash, but then...

Darkness.

"... refuse to acknowledge that we're trying to help, and have no reason to work against your interests. The queen cares about Harmony, and does not wish to interfere with her start to life any more than she would with any other girl."

A deep, fatigued sigh reached Harmony's ears, and she slowly began to feel the sensation of sheets around her, and a pillow behind her.

"But we... cannot keep risking this much longer. At least, not without training her. It's a threat to your life, that of others, and hers too. If she doesn't take her medicine just one more time... I don't know whether I'll be able to stand here and give you another chance, Daku. It was already incredibly lucky that I was nearby to handle the damage and bring her here."

"I-Irin...?"

Groaning out loud, Harmony slowly sat up in bed. Flickering memories filled her mind – of the day where she had first experienced her powers, and had met Irin. And, later, of the store.

What have I done?

Her eyes jolted open in guilt, but no sooner had she done so, than she was caught up in a hug from her father, and could see a figure standing just behind him – not Yuuto this time, like when she'd fainted in the forest, but Kijury, dressed in his usual cloths and looking deeply concerned.

"Oh, thank Ophin..." After a few moments, Daku broke out of the hug with a frown. "Harmony, why did you lie to me?"

Her face fell, and she looked away from her father. "I just wanted to control my powers... If I did, then you and Kijury wouldn't have to be scared, and I could stay with you..." She looked up and over at Kijury. "What happened? And where's Irin? Is she... okay?"

"Irin is at home, unscathed. And Archer... is alive, at least." the deer replied.

Harmony's eyes widened, filling with tears. "I-I didn't mean to do any of that... I don't know... what happened."

At this, Daku got up and walked over to Harmony's table, reaching for the box of black vials. "Harmony, just drink your medicine and-"

"Now, hold on a second, Daku." Kijury cut him off.

Harmony had tears falling from her eyes, and Kijury reached over to place a gentle hand on her shoulder. "Listen, Harmony. I'm sure you did not mean any harm to Archer. I got him to the hospital, and he is getting cared for as we speak."

"Really?" Harmony asked pleadingly.

But though her face showed nothing but fear and concern, she could feel the voices inside tugging in a different direction altogether. *If he lives... He'll tell everyone about you stealing. You should have finished the job.*

The deer nodded. "This wasn't your fault. But if you want to stop it from happening again sometime, then there is only one way that we can help you."

Daku bristled at this, glaring from across the room. "Enough. You have tried me far more than you have any right to, today."

Kijury's eyes flickered over to him with a glare. "Daku."

The male cat's mouth snapped shut, and Kijury took the chance to look back over to Harmony. "I'd like to offer you to come train with us. In the Penlight castle. Myself and the other knights can help you learn to control your powers."

Still visibly torn, Daku stepped back towards the bed and reached out urgently – almost as though he wanted to take his daughter's hand – but then stopped short. "Harmony... please. The kingdom, the knights... have never brought any-thing but pain to our family. I can't let you suffer the same fate."

"But Dad..." The girl shook her head, speaking with passion. "I don't want to hurt anyone again. I want to protect others."

Kijury solemnly inclined his head in her direction. "So, is that a yes?"

Harmony looked from the deer to her father, then back to Kijury – her head spinning, crazy, new ideas forming, and a fresh, enthusiastic determination filling her.

"Yes. I... want to learn."

4

They fear you, Harmony. They want you dead! Kill them all, before it's too late!

Harmony sat up quickly in her bed – glancing about the dimly lit room, and feeling dark energy swirling about her head tangibly. *The voices...* She thought. *I don't like them at all... Are they part of what Kijury was telling me I could learn to control? I sure hope so.*

But then the thought of yesterday's conversation with the deer knight came back to her, and her mind began to race with excitement. *Today's the day!*

A few seconds later she was on her feet, taking her daily sip from one of the black vials, dressing into casual clothes, and walking out of her room and into the kitchen. When she passed through the threshold, she saw her father already sitting at the table – head held in his hands, and a single plate of salad in front of him, clearly not intended for the male cat himself.

"Hey, Dad!" she meowed.

Daku looked up from the table to recognize Harmony's arrival. "Hey, Harmony." His voice was solemn.

Harmony, however, gave him a bright smile, sat down, and began to eat her salad. "Thanks, Dad!"

Her father nodded and sighed in response, looking away from her as he sat down at the table next to her.

For a while Harmony simply ate, but then the silence began to get to her, and she frowned deeply while looking at her father. *This is about the training.*

She paused, and softened her face. "I'll be fine, Dad."

Daku remained silent for a few further seconds, before looking back at this daughter and holding her gaze. "I just don't want you to get hurt. Just please, be careful, Harmony,"

Harmony let out a sigh, looking down at what was left of her salad. *Why does Dad hate the kingdom?* "Of course not. I'll be more careful than ever."

Letting his daughter out of the hug with great difficulty, Daku forced a smile, and nodded his head. "Then have fun."

Harmony positively beaned in response. "I will, Dad. Thanks!"

At that moment, however, they heard a knock at the door. *That must be Kijury!*

Pushing away from her father completely, Harmony ran over to the door and pulled it open to see a familiar, cloak-clad deer standing in the threshold with a wooden staff in hand.

"Hello, Harmony," Kijury greeted her with a smile, before glancing over her shoulder at Daku and bidding the older cat a terse half-nod. "Are you prepared to head to the castle?"

She nodded, and stepped through the doorway to join Kijury on the cobble outside. "Yep!"

Daku moved forward to watch through the doorway as the two walked a few paces away, and Harmony glanced up at the deer once more. "Which way are we taking for the walk?"

Kijury chuckled, and tapped his staff on the ground. "None of them."

Harmony quirked her head to the side. "Then how are we..."

She was suddenly cut off as she and Kijury disappeared in a puff of greenish, blueish fog that quickly dispersed into the morning air.

Closing his eyes tightly and returning inside, Daku first visited the kitchen, pulled a bottle of wine from a high shelf, and uncorked it before moving to the living room and sitting on the couch to take a long, deep sip. *My wife is dead... My daughter is walking in her footsteps...*

Tilting the bottle back down and wiping the fur around his lips, he sighed deeply.

"I just have to hope nothing goes wrong,"

"...going to get there?"

The feeling was... unbelievably strange. Being in one place at one moment, and in a completely different one in the next. At first she was almost disorientated enough to lose her footing, but then the world stopped spinning, and she found herself glancing up and around at a grand, stone hall with a long carpet, and colorful banners interchanging with sunlit windows lining its walls.

The space was largely empty, but what furnishings there were – plush chairs, oil paintings, and glass cases – were ornate and well-kept, and Harmony didn't think she'd ever been in a place that was more sophisticated, nor that felt more foreign to her and the humble village she'd grown up in.

"Harmony!" a feminine voice called nearby.

The girl's head jerked around, and then her eyes bugged wide open as she saw a familiar face dashing towards her. *Irin?*

It was indeed the red dragon girl – a wide smile across her face, and her arms already open to wrap Harmony up in one of her usual hugs.

Harmony blinked in surprise as she returned the embrace. "What are you doing here?!"

The dragon girl giggled. "Kijury brought me here! He said I get to study and learn how to control my powers too!"

"I thought it might be better to keep things a surprise." Kijury walked past the two with a bright smile. "But now come with me. I'll explain more soon.

Looking at each other gleefully, the girls followed after the staff-wielding deer as they turned down into a long hall. There were a series of doors along the way – with most of them being open, but one smaller set at the latter end of the hall being closed.

"What's in that room?" Harmony questioned, pointing at the closed door.

Kijury turned around for a second to glance back, still walking. "That's the queen's quarters."

"Oh!" the girls said in unison.

The three continued down the hall past a number of further doorways, until they arrived at a set of large, curved wooden doors. Kijury tapped the top of his staff in between the doors, and an ice-blue aura shone between them shortly afterwards – parting them, and allowing them to pass through.

"This is so cool!" Harmony meowed in excitement.

Irin nodded rapidly. "Yeah! Imagine we can do that, one day!"

Kijury chuckled at this, but continued to lead the way through the doorway out into a large, square yard – ringed by small parapets of stone, stood under the open sky above, and with a floor that was partially grass and stone.

The cat girl glanced around in awe at the well-kept size of the place, wondering which part of the palace this courtyard made up, and seeing a number of small towers and other sections of the castle in the near distance.

"This is where you two will train." Kijury explained, turning to face the two teens. "You will learn to use your powers in a controlled environment, and I will be here to assist and keep things under control."

Harmony listened with her jaw slack in amazement, and then nodded. "When do we get to start?"

The deer smiled, and tapped the end of his staff on the stones beneath him. "First, let's get you two into proper clothing."

A cyan line of energy flowed from the staff – splitting in two, and ranging over to the feet of the two girls, where it slowly began to envelop their ankles, legs, and lower bodies until it reached all the way to their shoulders.

Harmony and Irin almost staggered back in surprise, but before they could express confusion as to what was happening, the energy faded darker, and soon turned into tangible, visible fabric – a full training uniform with padding in vulnerable places, and a light chest piece that settled well across their shoulders. Finally, the energy dissipated about their waists, leaving them each with simple belts and small pouches attached.

"Woah! These look amazing!" Harmony meowed, reaching down to pat at her new, mystically summoned attire.

"And they are yours to keep," Kijury stated.

"Really?!" the two friends yelled in unison.

"Indeed!" Kijury chuckled. "But now... first things first." he stepped back, and gestured for the two girls to do the same. "We will spar a little, with what you know of your abilities. But be careful."

Irin nodded. "Okay!"

Harmony looked confused at first, but then smiled and turned about to take a few steps away from her friend. "Got it!"

Soon, the two girls were facing one another in loose, awkward fighting stances, with Kijury still watching over to the side. Harmony had her fists up, and an unsure expression on her face. "I-I won't go easy on you!"

Kijury gave a nod to indicate that they could commence, but while Irin responded to this by starting to rock from foot to foot in expectation of their spar getting started, Harmony froze completely – finding herself suddenly caught unaware by a dark voice echoing through her head. *This is your first chance to prove yourself, Harmony. Let me take over.*

"Stay out of this..." she mumbled, closing her eyes, and ignoring its words – instead starting to move forward towards Irin.

At first her pace was slow and unsure, but then the energy welling up within her began to manifest in a low growl, and her arms began to surge with dark energy.

Kijury's eyes widened, and his staff glowed with blue light. "Harmony?"

Without warning, the cat was suddenly lunging forward towards her friend. Irin tried to dodge out of the way, but leaned forward with her head clumsily in doing so, and caught the cat's fist against the side of her skull as a result – sending her stumbling back with a cry.

Coming to crouch with a growl, Harmony glared over at her staggering friend and Kijury in quick, angry succession. Her fur was sticking up, and when she spoke, it didn't really seem as though she was addressing the two before her. "Leave me alone!"

"Harmony, calm yourself! Think about what you're doing, you can control this!" the deer shouted, pointing his staff at her now. "And Ishii – don't lead with your head."

Irin nodded and scrambled to a sitting position, but Harmony didn't show any sign of understanding whatsoever – paws glowing black, and eyes flicking up to stay on Kijury. The deer had only a sliver of a second to react before her hands followed, and a blast of dark came with them – darting towards him only to be dissolved by a shield of green.

Kijury didn't hesitate to act whatsoever from then on, however. Stepping to the side, hefting his staff, and tapping it on the ground twice, he send his shield flying towards Harmony before she could strike again, and it waved over her like a mist – first confusing the cat girl, then causing her darkened eyes to flicker, and her body to slowly slump unconscious to the ground.

"Sorry, Harmony. At least your power is still easy enough to subdue." Kijury apologized under his breath, before looking over at Irin still sitting where she had landed with a shocked expression on her face.

"But we have a lot of training to get through..."

Later, in the evening, after Kijury had brought her home and Daku had administered her medicine, Harmony lay in her bed staring at her paws.

I wanted to control my powers. To not hurt anyone again. And now I... hurt Irin. What if she hates me? I just don't understand why I'm like this.

At that moment, Daku's head poked in through the bedroom doorway, and he met Harmony's gaze with a weak, strained smile. He hadn't taken the incident earlier well, and it was clear that he was still tense about it. "Just wanted to check whether there's anything you need before sleep."

"I'm fine, I guess, but..." Harmony rubbed at the back of her head, and looked down at the sheets. "I wanted to ask... where did my powers come from?"

The cat man frowned. "You need to recover, Harmony. Especially if you want to continue with... training tomorrow. Keep these silly questions for later."

"Did Mom have powers?"

His face remained as impassive as stone. "Rest, Harmony. It's getting late."

Harmony sighed and nodded in response – resulting in her Dad ducking back from the doorway and his footsteps trailing away. *Does this mean... that I'm right? Or does he just not know what to say.*

I just know that I hope I find out, one day. The sooner, the better.

5

Harmony slept restlessly – questions, guilt, and hopes for what training could hold in the future swirling through her head without reprieve.

The morning provided little relief to her mix of uncertainty, fear, and persistent excitement, especially with her father trading little words with her other than to bid her a good day, and this tension only grew when Kijury knocked at the door, took her arm, and vanished with her to appear back at the Penlight Palace's training field once more.

Irin was already standing by the exit out into the field in her training uniform when they arrived, and Harmony wasted no time in breaking away from Kijury's side and dashing towards her to wrap the dragon up in a hug. "Irin!"

The two embraced for a few seconds before the cat brought out with a frown. "I'm sorry for hurting you yesterday... I didn't mean to!"

The dragon girl giggled, not a sliver of resentment on her face. "It's okay! It's just training!"

"I'll control it, I promise you!" Harmony assured her friend.

Kijury nodded from off to the side. "I know you will, Harmony. It'll take time, though. And training. Speaking of which – are you two ready?"

Smiles on their faces, the girls nodded.

Kijury smiled back, and led the two out through the doors and into the daylight of the training field itself.

Harmony turned to her friend as they made out into the field's center. "Do your parents have powers, Irin?"

The dragon shrugged. "My Dad does, but only a little. He uses them to help moving and shaping stone."

"Wow!" Harmony's enthusiasm remained, but her brain wandered. *I wonder if Dad has powers? Or my Mom?*

Kijury halted in his tracks in the middle of the area, turning to glance back at Irin with his staff held out in front of him. "Have you practiced what I taught you?"

Irin nodded. "Yes!"

Harmony glanced confusedly at Kijury, and then at her friend. "Huh?"

"Show Harmony, Irin." The deer instructed.

The dragon nodded. She opened her claws, closed her eyes, and took a deep breath. Rocks slowly started to form in her palms, and soon covered her claws – making it about halfway up her wrists before they stopped, and Irin was left panting but excited. "I did it!"

Harmony's eyes were wide with thrill. "Woah! Irin, that's amazing!"

"Well done, Irin," Kijury praised. "Now we'll spar again – but Harmony, I want you to keep yourself under control, okay?"

Nodding, Harmony stepped away from Irin and assumed a fighting stance with fists up. "I'll try my best!"

Irin copied her friend's stance. "Ready when you are, Harmony!"

Harmony looked down at her right fist, which was glowing with its usual black aura, before glancing back up at her friend and taking a few deep breaths to try to keep herself under control. *I got this...*

Kijury stood close to the two, staff ready, and gave a single nod to indicate that they could start.

Harmony sprinted toward Irin as soon as the signal was given, readying a strike with her right arm. "Take this!" she shouted.

Irin ducked and struck Harmony in the gut with her left fist. "Gotcha!" she beamed in satisfaction.

The cat girl staggered back hard from the punch, almost losing her balance, and ending up bent over and holding her stomach.

Irin gasped, nearly running over to her friend. "Are you okay, Harmony?!"

"She'll get through it, Irin, keep going," Kijury called from the sidelines.

Nodding, the dragon exhaled, putting her fists up again and charging once more. Harmony stood back up straight in response, a frown forming on her face. *I have to do better... I'm stronger than this.*

Clenching her fists, Harmony mirrored the charge with equal energy – meeting the dragon's advance with a strong blast of darkness. The dragon ducked out of the way easily, only to then get hit by another bolt from Harmony's left paw.

Irin staggered backward, though still with a smile on her face. "Nice one, Harmony!"

But the cat wasn't done. "Take this!" Harmony shouted, throwing two fresh arcane blows outwards.

The dragon gasped, but successfully blocked both strikes with her rock covered claws – though not without losing some of their covering.

"Keep going, you two! You're doing wonderful!" Kijury cheered the girls on.

Irin's left arm covered itself with smaller, finer stones, and she lashed out with it toward Harmony – sending the stones flying in her direction. The black aura around Harmony only flashed for a moment, however, and sent them right back at Irin. Reacting almost too late, Irin's eyes widened, and she summoned a small wall in front of her to take the shower of small blows.

"That won't get me, Irin!" Harmony exclaimed, dashing towards her friend again.

The dragon girl raised both arms, summoning another wall of stone before her, anticipating a frontal blow, but after a few seconds... it never came, and she was suddenly struck from behind by a blast of energy – sending her staggering forward, and just barely catching herself from landing face-first into her dispelling magic rock. Harmony had dodged around her while she was blinded.

"Excellent job, Harmony!" Kijury raised his voice in praise from off to the side once more.

The energy surrounding Harmony's arms faded as she knelt, panting, beside her friend to help Irin up. The dragon had a wide smile across her face as soon as she got into a sitting position. "That... was so freaking cool!" she gushed and giggled. "You're amazing."

"Are you sure I didn't hurt you?" The cat girl frowned.

Irin nodded, smiling at Harmony. "I'm fine! And, remember, you're learning. Next time, you'll have control over it – I know you will!"

The cat girl giggled, deeply relieved. "Thanks, Irin! You're the best!"

The two hugged closely on their knees, and Kijury chuckled at the sight. "How sweet. We'll take a break for now, though, girls – I'll get something to eat for lunch before we continue."

"Yes!" the girls cheered in unison, though they remained hugging for a long second afterwards.

I'll control my powers... I'll control them, and keep everyone safe.

Mase watched the two girls leave the training field from an open castle window – face impassive, but eyes alert and sincere. *She can barely control her powers, even now. Is training her like this reducing the danger, or simply teaching her skills she will use against us in the end?*

He sighed exasperatedly. "Ophin watch over Penlight..."

"He's always watching over us, Mase. He sees everything, and guides us all," a voice said from behind him.

Rolling his eyes somewhat, Mase shifted about to glance behind himself. Illusionary was stood at the back of the small study room the fire knight had been inhabiting for the morning with his arms folded in the lap of his robe, and a wide smile on the cheetah's face.

"I assume you're worried about Harmony," the feline voiced.

"Is it *that* obvious?" Mase growled.

"Yes, it's that obvious," Illusionary chuckled. "But I understand your concern."

Mase furrowed his brow at Illusionary, then glanced back outside the window. The three were gone, now, leaving only the scars on the grass and stone of the training yard as evidence of their practice. "She can't control her powers. I think it is well known that I wasn't... fond of Tsuki. But when it comes to her girl... I don't wish to see the situation repeat itself. Let alone imagine the damage she could do to the kingdom if we aren't there to put an end to things, need be."

"Have faith, Mase. In Kijury, and our lord Ophin above all." Illusionary shook his head as he preached. "Not to mention my medicine. Do you not trust that, at least, to achieve all, all the ends we have here?"

The flaming knight stared at the cheetah for a few heartbeats before nodding. "As you say."

Illusionary shrugged his shoulders, turned about, and walked to the room's wooden door. "If you ever wish to pray with me at my church, then you would be most welcome. But for now, I will leave you to your thoughts. Waiting, after all, is often the boldest kind of action."

Mase closed his eyes, feeling the breeze through the window on his face.

As much as I hate to admit it... there's nobody better for the job than you, Kijury. If anyone can stop us from having to put her down, as distasteful as that would be... it's you.

6

Sat at the kitchen table in her house, Harmony finished up her morning salad, smiled, and got up from the table to do away with her bowl and fork. *Ready for the day. Can't believe we're going to go visit the Ishii family before training today!*

The cat girl already had her training uniform on, and was only waiting for her father to come downstairs and walk to the castle with her, and so now decided to use the time waiting to practice a little. Taking a deep breath in and out, she punched the air steadily, and tried to summon a moderate, controllable amount of energy into each strike. *I've got this!*

As her success seemed to increase, and the darkness around her paws remained at a management level, she moved faster and faster. *One day I can master all my abilities. Maybe even teleport, like Kijury said I can learn to!*

"Harmony?"

She whipped around to see her father standing in the door, and gave him a nervous smile – embarrassed that he had seen her boxing the air. "Oh, hey, Dad!"

He sighed a little, but made no comment. "Are you ready to go? We were supposed to be at the Ishii's ten minutes ago already."

Harmony nodded, and made to follow her father as he walked through the living room, to the front door, and out onto the village path.

Their journey out of the village was a quiet, undisturbed one, and it only took them a quarter of an hour or so to leave the trees and fields for the slowly more and more densely populated outskirts of the castle.

Before long they completely surrounded by urban bustle, and Harmony was beaming as usual at seeing the life and excitement of it all. That was when, however, they took a corner, and her eyes fell upon the damaged, partially ruined façade of Penlight Petty Trade.

The girl's feet ground to a halt on the cobble, and she gasped out loud before covering her mouth with her paws. *I... did that? And the nice snake... I hope he's okay. I haven't even checked in on him.*

"Harmony."

She looked to her right to see her father looking down upon her, and a tear fell from the corner of her eye. "I-I didn't mean to hurt him, Dad..."

Daku moved in to give Harmony a tight hug, stroking her hair. "I know. And he's fine. I'm sure... whatever Kijury is teaching you will help, at least a little. As long as you keep taking your medicine."

A while later, after Harmony had her fill of the hug, they continued walking. It wasn't long before the next building of interest appeared, however – a tall, stately manor with a large holy symbol above its door, that was right next to the castle's largest church to Ophin.

They must love the church! She let out a tiny giggle.

Daku looked over at his daughter again at the noise. "What's so funny?"

She pointed over at the manor. "They live next to the church!"

That brought a sudden drop in mood and openness from her father, rather than the compassion he had exhibited earlier. "That's where the high priest lives."

"Oh... will I get to meet him?" Harmony asked. "What's his name?"

Yet Daku declined to answer or meet his daughter's eyes – instead reaching over to tug on her hand and speeding up his pace forward. "Enough. We don't want to be late."

Harmony followed dutifully, although a little reluctantly, and moments later they arrived in front of a red, black, wooden store with the small windows of an apartment lined up on its second story. There was a sign next to it that read 'Ishii Stone Market'.

The cat girl was positively bursting with excitement at the sign and the thought of seeing her best friend, but her father seemed still quite somber as he pushed the door to the store open, and led them both inside.

Her excitement before, however, was nothing compared to that which she felt upon taking in the crowded, ornate contents of the store itself. There were well carved sculptures, pillars, and structural pieces everywhere her eyes could see – leaned up against the wall, on platforms on the floor, and even hanging from the ceiling.

Her jaw dropped. "This place is so cool!"

But before she could say more or take in any more details, there was a great kerfuffle of noise from the stairs to the left of the door, and the two felines turned about just in time to be barraged into by a trio of larger, scaled forms. "Look out below!"

First it was Dorthro – snatching up Daku into a tight embrace as usual. Then it was the big dragon's wife, Anahita, who gave a friendly wave and a light squeeze on Harmony's shoulder. And last but not least – Irin, also already in her training uniform, and rushed forward to wrap her best friend up in her arms as was customary for them. "Good morning, Harmony!"

"Good morning to you too!" Harmony purred back, as her father was finally released from Dorthro's embrace, and the five eventually came to regard one another properly.

Irin was the first to speak up again. "Are you ready to go?"

Harmony nodded. "Yeah!" She turned to her father. "But before we go – when training is over, can we have a sleepover? Please!"

Daku sighed, seeming less than invigorated by the enthusiastic greeting. "If Irin's parents are…"

Dorthro was nodding enthusiastically before Daku could even finish speaking. "We sure are. You two can stay as long as you'd like!"

"Yay!" the girls cheered in unison, turning to one another with wide smiles.

At that moment, however, there was a knock on the shop's door.

Everyone in the room turned towards the door, and shortly after it cracked open to show a smiling cervine face.

"Kijury!" All the dragons shouted, exhibiting quite some joy, while Daku's face merely fell further at the sight of the deer.

Slipping inside properly, the deer waved. "Hello, everyone! I see that it's not just Irin here today but Harmony, too!" He bowed his head. "But unfortunately, I'm not just here for a social visit."

"Training time?" Irin questioned.

Kijury nodded, and turned to the three parents standing before him. "I'll be back with them later! Have a lovely day, in the meantime."

"Bye, Dad!" Harmony meowed, before following Kijury and her friend out through the door and back into the bright day outside.

"Begin." Kijury tapped his staff twice on the ground.

With an enthusiastic cry, Harmony dashed forward across the training yard floor towards Irin for what felt like the tenth time that week – narrowly dodging her friend's first punch with an ease that had definitely gotten smoother over the days, and retaliating with a pulse of dark energy into the dragon's stomach.

The dragon slid back on the ground as a result, but Harmony was quick to close the gap – continuing her rush and doing her best to lash out with more arcane blows. Yet Irin had her arms up and stone barriers formed in front of each – deflecting the force of her magic easily and pushing her back quite some feet with her own power.

Kijury watched the girls fight from a safe distance with an impressed expression. "They've made wonderful progress the past few days," he uttered to himself.

Growling playfully, Harmony pushed herself back onto steady feet once more, concentrated as hard as she could, closed her eyes, and raised both arms in front of her. "Take this!"

A thick, powerful pillar of energy streamed from her paws – shooting towards Irin, and almost not giving her enough time for her to react – her reflexive shield shattering into pieces through deflecting the blow.

As the rain of small stones fell down about him, Kijury tapped his staff on the ground, and created a misty green shield of his own to protect himself. But although the move had been impressive, the voices in Harmony's head were far from satisfied. *Too weak. Faster. Harder. Strike to kill.*

Harmony tossed her head, and growled under her breath. "Leave me alone."

But the effect had already taken place. She could feel anger and dark energy welling up within her arms and chest – a familiar kind, although one that she had been successfully coming to feel less and less through training – and her next move was far more aggressive than those before.

The cat leaped forward before Irin could fully recover from the strength of the blow she had just defended herself against – landing one punch on her arm, and then another on her chest with enough strength to send the dragon girl falling backwards onto her tail.

At first Harmony intended to stop herself there – their sparring rules dictated that being downed was grounds enough for a pause – but she felt almost as though she had no control, by that point. Stepping over to loom over the downed girl, she raised her hand to deal another blow to Irin's chest.

Again! the voice ordered. But before her arm could lash down again, there was a tight wrapping about her wrist, and she glanced up with sudden clarity to see Kijury's hand stopping her.

The deer's eyebrow raised, and the staff in his other hand glistened with energy. "Having fun there, Harmony?"

A few seconds passed as Harmony panted, Irin scrambled back on the stone floor and groaned a little in pain, and Kijury shook his head – watching her eyes closely to ensure that they were clearing of darkness, and that the cat girl was regaining control. "That isn't an enemy, Harmony. That's your friend, Irin. Remember?"

Harmony looked over at Irin, who was still nursing her sore chest. "Oh, my god..." she whispered, pulling her hand away from the deer and scrambling over to the dragon, tears falling down her face.

"I-I got carried away... Are you okay?" Harmony asked in a shaky tone.

Irin was breathing hard, and took a moment to speak, but nodded her head nonetheless and seemed to be more or less recovering. "M-mhm! I'm fine!"

"Are you sure?" Kijury approached the two with concern. "That was... quite the hit."

Irin nodded, looking over at Kijury now. "After the first punch, I turned the scales on my stomach into stone. Though Harmony's punches still hit hard!"

Breaking out of the hug, the cat wiped the tears from her eyes. "Your punches hurt a lot, too!"

Kijury smiled, seeming relieved. "We'll take a break for a moment, let both of you make sure that you're alright."

Standing up and still breathing hard, the two walked over to one of the stone walls at the edge of the training yard and leant against it to catch their breath, with Kijury standing nearby. Irin looked over at their mentor. "Are we doing good?"

Kijury nodded. "You both are doing excellent! But let's not shake up the castle or one another," he chuckled.

The dragon giggled, looking beyond pleased, but although Harmon was smiling as well, her look soon switched to confusion as she saw someone walking up behind Kijury.

Kijury noticed the confusion on the cat's face. "Something wrong, Harmony?"

"Who's that?" Harmony pointed behind the deer.

Kijury turned about to glance where she was pointing, and his eyes widened. Approaching them at a graceful, measured pace was a blonde-furred hound with golden, almost fiery hair and a tail the flicked with each step.

Irin's mouth drifted open. "She's so pretty!"

Harmony nodded in agreement. *Is she... the queen? What could she possibly want from us?*

"M'lady!" Kijury bent a knee to her briefly, before shifting about and gesturing urgently to the children behind him. "Please, bow for our queen."

Both Harmony and Irin obeyed immediately, although a little nervously, but as soon as they had, the queen spoke up in a gentle, kind tone. "Thank you, Kijury. But that won't be necessary. You may stand."

The hound woman smiled, looking the two girls across from her up and down. "You two must be Harmony Mei and Irin Ishii, correct?"

They both nodded, and Irin spoke up dutifully. "Yes, m'lady!"

"Just call me Upholder, girls," the queen told them.

"If I may ask, m'lady, do you need anything?" Kijury spoke up once more.

"I'm here to watch the girls train," Upholder explained, though there was something a little more than casual interest in her tone and demeanor now.

"Is that so!" Kijury blinked, and then looked back over at Harmony and Irin. "Well – in that case, I have something different in mind." He smirked a little. "Do you feel ready to take on me for a change, girls?"

Both Harmony's and Irin's eyes widened in surprise. "Spar against you?!" they exclaimed.

The deer nodded, and Harmony's jaw dropped. "I g-guess so!"

"Good! Go to one side of the yard then. I'll go to the other." Kijury said, before walking off back into the center of the training field.

Harmony looked over at Upholder, unsure quite what was happening, and the queen gave her a smile in return. *She smiled at me!*

But then the two were rushing away to take their places, and Irin was turning to her best friend with concern. "Do you really think we can beat Kijury?"

Harmony nodded with pride. "I don't see why not! We can at least give it a try."

Irin's look of disbelief switched to a wide smile. "You're right. Let's give it our best!"

They turned to face Kijury, who was a few feet away from them – putting their fists up, and preparing to use their powers. Harmony's paws began to glow with their usual black aura, and Irin's claws, arms, legs, and feet began to reinforce themselves with stone.

The girls watched as Kijury spun his staff from his right hand to his left, then back to his right again. "Begin!"

Harmony was the first to move, as she often was during their sparring – letting out blast after blast of dark energy. This continued for some time, with Irin getting up close and trying to land a melee blow, while Kijury cast protective fields of green that repelled both her advances and the cat girl's arcane orbs with apparent ease.

Eventually, however, one of Harmony's blasts very nearly did make it through the deer's guard, and he was sent into a light stagger with his staff sagging in one hand, and the other raised to call off the combat. "That's enough."

The girls immediately snapped out of their fighting positions, and stood there panting a little as Kijury recovered his footing and nodded proudly. "Nearly."

"You two are doing excellent so far," Upholder praised the girls, moving over from where she had been watching.

"Thank you, Upholder!" Harmony and Irin said in unison, somewhat breathless.

"Now keep this in mind," Upholder started. "You are not training just to control your abilities – through this path, you two can also become knights of the Penlight Kingdom. To serve alongside the other knights, and Kijury, to protect our people."

"We can become what?!" Harmony and Irin exclaimed in unison. The dragon turned to her best friend. "Isn't that exciting, Harmony?"

Harmony's shock turned to a frown. "My Dad might not like it... he doesn't like the kingdom, though I don't know why."

Irin frowned too. "I'm sure it will be alright... I think my parents would love to hear that I could grow up to do something so grand!"

The queen nodded direly at this. "I understand. At any rate, you still have training to do. And when the time comes, we will see what happens."

Kijury and Upholder began to talk, then, and Harmony lowered her gaze to the floor, caught up in thoughts of her powers, her dad, and the future.

I hope you're right, Irin, I really do.

A few hours later, Harmony and Irin finished their training for the day, and traced their way back to the Ishii Stone Shop under the early evening sky.

Daku had left for his own house not long ago, after giving Harmony permission to stay for the night, and as such the two girls were soon upstairs in Irin's room making things comfortable for themselves. Harmony sat atop Irin's bed in a white shirt and black shorts, and Irin stood in the center of the daintily-furnished room in an orange blouse.

"I'm going to go see if there're more pillows!" the dragon said, ducking off through the door leading out into the lounge.

Harmony nodded and smiled. "Okay! Sounds good!"

Then she was gone, and Harmony laid back onto the dragon's bed. *Today was super fun! And I can't believe we're getting a sleepover.*

Now imagine how fun it could be if you really used your powers! You almost did it, we're so proud of you.

Harmony sat up like a rocket, gulping hard at the unexpected intrusion of the dark, hidden voices. "No... She put a paw on the side of her head. "Please, go away... everything's fine..."

"Harmony! I found two pillows!" Irin called from the living room, interrupting both any further noise from the voices and Harmony's own discomfort.

The cat's head whipped about and the energy beginning to well up in her arms drained out as Irin ran into the room a pillow in each hand – arms raised to toss them. "Catch!"

Harmony caught one pillow, but another hit her in the face and almost knocked her back on the bed. "Woah!"

"Oh, sorry!" Irin hopped onto the bed next to Harmony, giving her a hug as she recovered her balance.

Embracing it, Harmony nuzzled her friend. "It's okay. I already know you have terrible aim from training."

Pushing back, Irin picked up one of the pillows, and jokingly furrowed her brow. "Oh, you're in for it now!"

But Harmony was quicker – grabbing up the other, and whipping it about so that it caught her friend on the snout before she could even prepare her first strike.

And so the pillow fight began – ranging on for some time until both girls were sore, dead tired, and passed out next to one another on the sheets.

By the time that the morning came, when the sunny, peaceful day outside was slowly coming to a light bustle, Harmony found herself tossing and turning in Irin's bed. Her face was contorted, and her body shaky and sweaty. "N-No..."

Yes! Let us take over!

"No!" Harmony shouted and sat up awake – rubbing at her face until the pressure from inside her mind and the buzzing of dark energy went away.

Irin shot up next to her – groggy at first, but then confused and distressed at the messy, panting state her friend was in. "Huh?! Harmony? Are you okay?" She reached over and pulled her friend into a sidelong hug.

Embracing the hug, the cat girl nodded and tried to ground herself. "Y-Yeah... just a nightmare..."

"Well, it's all over now! No need to worry!" The dragon reassured her.

"Well, good morning! What are you girls up to with that noise?"

Jolting up out of their embrace, the girls looked across the room to see the door cracked open a little, and Irin's mother Anahita standing there with a wide smile on her friendly face.

"Morning, Mrs. Ishii!" Harmony meowed, pulling back from Irin to yawn and stretch her arms. *I feel like I didn't sleep much at all.*

Anahita smiled. "Good morning. Dorthro is cooking breakfast. Will you join us, Harmony?"

"Of course I will!" Irin answered for her – scrambling out of the bed.

Anahita left the doorway with a chuckle, with Irin following soon after, and Harmony hooping out of bed in turn. A short walk down the hall and the morning light-lit lounge later and they were in the family kitchen – a cozy, humbly decorated space that had windows showing out onto the street below, and a small table with enough space for four.

On the other side of the kitchen, Dorthro, with a chef's hat and apron on, flipped pancakes idly while turning back to face the three new arrivals with a chuckle. "Good morning, ladies!"

"Morning, Mr. Ishii!" Harmony mewled.

Anahita walked over to Dorthro, kissing him on the cheek. "Good morning!"

He turned back to the stove, flipping pancakes onto plates one after the other. "Now take a seat! It's breakfast time!"

Irin and Harmony ran over to the table, with the cat girl sitting directly in front of the window, and Anahita moved slowly to sit across from them. A few moments later the table was steadily filled with full plates, and Dorthro himself flopped down onto the last chair with a grin – immediately receiving a kiss on the lips from his wife upon doing so.

"It looks delicious, Dad!" Irin licked her lips, and Harmony nodded in agreement.

Soon enough, Harmony and the Ishii family dug in, with Irin keeping bright smile on her face as she ate with her best friend.

Harmony smiled as well – although there was a slight bittersweet edge to the brightness in her heart. *So this is what it's like to sit together with a family.*

In that moment, she didn't think she'd missed her Mom more in her entire life.

7

Long day after long day of training filled Harmony and Irin's weeks – with Kijury coming to fetch them from their respective houses every morning, and the two girls then walking back through the city and, in Harmony's case, back to the village every evening.

Time went on in this fashion, until around two months had passed since they first started training. On this particular evening, the sun was even more bright and golden in the sky than usual, and the Irin and Harmony had even wider smiles than usual too upon arriving at the Ishii Stone Shop – slipping through the door in quick succession only to be promptly greeted by and hugged by the dragon's father.

"How was training today, hmm?" Dorthro rumbled, letting go of his daughter and stepping back with a smile.

"It was super fun! We're both getting so strong. Harmony nearly knocked me out!" Irin replied.

"Oh, really now?" Dorthro set his eyes on the cat girl.

Harmony chuckled nervously. "Yeah! I got a little carried away..."

"Wonderful!" Surprising her by pulling her into a tight hug as well, Dorthro chuckled. "It makes me happy that my little Irin has someone to grow big and strong with!"

Harmony lost air from Dorthroruth's hug. "O-Of course! I'll always be here for Irin. She's my best friend!"

Dorthro let go of Harmony and set her down. "Good! But I'm sure you girls don't want to talk about training after such a long day."

Now it was Irin's time to chuckle. "Nope!" She turned to her friend. "Are you staying the night again, Harmony?"

Harmony shook her head. "I wish I could, but Dad said I have to get back home right after training today..." She sighed, ears drooping.

"Aw..." Irin frowned.

"That's alright, Harmony. Maybe you can join us at the harvest festival tomorrow?" Dorthro suggested, cracking another cheerful smile.

The dragon girl's face lit back up immediately with a wide smile of her own. "Wonderful idea, Dad!"

Unable to keep from joining in with a grin, Harmony nodded eagerly. "I'll ask my Dad once I get home!" She leaned in and hugged her friend. "I hope we can go!"

"I hope so too!" Irin said, smiling, before Harmony pushed back and waved as she trotted towards the door through which they had just come.

"Goodbye for now, Harmony!" Dorthro called, waving back.

Irin waved as well. "Bye, Harmony! I can't wait to hang out tomorrow!"

A few steps later and she was closing the door behind her with a sigh and a frown on her face. *I hope Dad lets me go.*

The afternoon was well underway by the time that Harmony walked back to her village – trudging away from the trees, and over in the direction of her house as a calm wind gusted past.

"Hey, Harmony!"

Harmony turned around to a somewhat familiar black furred wolf with a leather apron and ocean blue eyes waving to her from a house just on the other side of the cobblestone road.

"Oh! Hey, Mr. Carnell!" Harmony responded with a smile – recognizing him as the town blacksmith. He and Daku had a complicated relationship, with the wolf's demeanor getting on the cat's nerves from time to time, but Harmony had still seem him around for almost as long as she could remember.

Leaning on his fence with a hearty chuckle, the wolf gave Harmony's uniform a look up and down. "You look like a mini knight straight from the kingdom!"

"Hah, yeah! I train there now!" Harmony meowed, pausing in her step.

"Really? That's great!" Mr. Carnell's tail wagged with genuine happiness. "Come to think of it, your mother used to train there too when she was your age, didn't she? Though I don't know what came of that."

The girl's eyes widened, and her jaw dropped in preparation to ask after, but then the wolf was turning about with a hand raised to bid farewell. "But as much as I'd love to stay – the wife will have my head if I don't get back inside to help with cooking. Sorry to head off so soon, but good luck with your training!"

She watched in disbelief as the blacksmith entered his house, shutting the door behind him. *I didn't know Mr. Carnell knew my Mom...*

Resuming along her way, Harmony soon arrived at her own house and stormed over to knock on the door. "Dad, I'm home! Let me in!"

The cat girl waited quite a few seconds, but no response came, so she gave another, firmer knock. "Dad?"

A long moment later, she heard someone slowly unlock the door, and eventually it opened to reveal her father stood beyond the threshold with short leggings on and no shirt. "Hey, Harmony..."

"Uh, hey, Dad..." Harmony responded, confused. Her father's voice was slurred, and the way he was holding himself made it clear that he was intoxicated.

He frowned and turned away from the door, seeming to leave it up to her to close it behind him. "How was training in that stupid place today."

"Are you okay, Dad?" Concerned, Harmony followed him in, and reached back to shut the door.

He started to answer her, but nearly tripped in entering the lounge, and she rushed to follow after – finding discarded bottles of alcohol stacked upon the lounge table. "Dad, are you drunk...?"

"Drunk?!" Standing in the center of the room, the male cat turned about. "Why would I be drunk?"

"Yes, you are!" Harmony moved forward to grab her father's paw, with leading him to his room on her mind, but stopped short. This… could be her chance. And she had to know.

He swayed on his feet for a moment, before groggily tilting his head. "What's wrong, my beautiful daughter?"

One deep breath later, and she said it. "Was Mom a knight for the kingdom?"

For long moment, Daku didn't react. But when he did, it was with violent speed. Pulling back from his daughter, he snarled, and lashed his hand out reflexively to slap her across the side of the face. "How dare you ask me that? You know better!"

The girl's body flinched hard to the side with the impact, and a gasp of pain slipped from her lips. Tears fell from her eyes as she eventually looked up at her father.

No sooner had Daku seen those tears, than his expression switched instantly from anger to deep, shocked sadness as he realized what he'd done. "H-Harmony… I didn't…" He reached out his arms towards her. "I'm sorry…"

But Harmony wasn't having it for a second. She pushed her father away hard, causing him to stagger back several steps.

He recovered sloppily, still trying to reach out to her. "Harmony, I didn't mean to…" Tears fell down his face.

But Harmony was already turning tail to dart away in the direction of her room. "I don't care!"

The sound of her door slamming soon came, and Daku slid down from the wall to the floor, putting his face in his paws.

"I'm so sorry, Harmony… I just… can't do this to you…"

When Harmony woke the next morning, her eyes were still wet from tears. Slowly reaching up, she put a paw to her right cheek and rubbed at the slight soreness there. *I... don't want to think about last night, or Mom. I just want to spend time with Irin, and enjoy a day off.*

One slow, reluctant standing up and dose of her medicine later, Harmony walked out into the kitchen, where Daku sat at the table with his head in his hands.

The older cat glanced about nervously as his daughter entered – seeming unsure what to say for a moment before his mouth finally opened. "Morning."

A short, sharp breath from Harmony. "I'm going to the market festival with Irin today."

Daku tilted his head in Harmony's direction, using a forcedly cheery tone of voice. "Oh, sounds nice! Do you need me to come with..."

"No."

Her father breathed slowly, nodded, and then turned back to hang his head again. Harmony walked out of the room and back into her own to get dressed in simple, casual clothing, and then moved back out into the hall.

Daku had risen and was standing by the door, now, a worried, fatigued expression on his face. "Harmony, can we please talk..." He walked over to her as she approached, reaching a paw out to her shoulder.

But the cat girl wasn't having it for a second. She smacked her father's paw away, hissing at him. "No, we can't! Leave me alone!"

Fur bristling slightly with dark energy, Harmony walked over to the front door – opening it roughly and storming out with a slam.

Harmony's bad mood persisted well into her walk to the castle, and even after picking up Irin from her family's shop, but by the time that she and the dragon girl wound up at the outskirts of the festival itself, she found it impossibly hard to stay somber.

The familiar streets of the castle were now a different world altogether – loud, crowded, and lined with countless stalls, each bearing its own colorful cloths, and some even being strung together by long ropes of colored streamers.

The two girls were playfully chasing after one another through the feet of others before long, nearly barrowing over customers and storekeepers alike as they ran. After a while, however, they found themselves getting worn out, and eventually slowed to hug and catch their breaths.

"This is so much fun!" Harmony giggled.

"Mhm!" her friend nodded in agreement.

Harmony opened her mouth to suggest something they could do next, but before she could, something caught her eye in the near distance, and her eyes widened in shock. Irin followed her gaze, and hers soon followed suit.

Two familiar figures ducked behind one of the bright stalls with wide smiles on their faces – two figures they'd never expected to see outside of the castle – Upholder, and their mentor Kijury. Both were dressed in relatively casual clothes, and seemed quite secretive about their actions.

"Is that Kijury and the Queen?" the dragon asked. "What are they doing here without the knights?"

But then the two leaned close together, and both girls were struck speechless – jaws dropping as the queen kissed Kijury on the cheek. The deer blushed, turning his head away, and Upholder chuckled – tugging him back out from behind the stall and amongst the crowd once more.

Both Irin and Harmony burst out in shocked giggles after the two had disappeared, unable to believe what they had seen. "Urgh – that's almost as bad as when my Mom and Dad kiss," said Irin.

Eventually they too continued along their way – moving out to the mansion quarter, where the stalls were a little thinner, and they finally got some relief from the avalanche of sound crashing upon their ears.

Soon, they came to stand in front of a particularly grand manor that had old-style architecture, and seemed quite unkept to the point of obvious abandonment.

"It looks empty – maybe we should explore it?" Irin said.

Harmony giggled – a bit taken aback by the suggestion, but excited nonetheless. "Sure, I guess it can't hurt! Is the door unlocked?"

"I'm guessing it isn't…" Moving forward alongside her friend, Harmony reached her claw out to the manor's doorknob and grabbed onto it. She turned the knob, but the door turned out to be unlocked. "Huh?"

"Maybe someone does live here after all?" the cat questioned.

"I don't know, but they wouldn't leave their door unlocked, right?" Irin pondered out loud.

Harmony Mei! You will leave right now! The voice got louder.

Yet Harmony only doubled down on ignoring it. "That's true… then let's go in."

Nodding, Irin walked in first, with the cat following close behind. Together, they moved into a dark, plain, wooden hallway, with one shut door at the end of the hallway, and one threshold immediately to their left, lit only by the light streaming in through the windows on the wall through which they had entered.

"This is creepy…" Irin stood close to Harmony as they drifted towards the nearest doorway.

"It's fine, Irin…" Harmony meowed, taking slow steps.

Just as they drew near to the threshold, however, there came a clear rustle from beyond the door in front of them, and the two girls froze. "Someone's down there, Harmony…" Irin's voice shook.

The cat nodded, but moved forward to push open the door anyway. It made an audible creaking sound as she pushed it all the way open, and behind it, she could see stairs that led down into a basement.

Harmony looked over at Irin, a little uneasy as well now. "Ready?"

Irin nodded cautiously.

Turning back about, Harmony walked down the steps with her dragon friend close in tow. Their progress was marked by a range of crackling from the steps themselves, and when they reached flat ground once more, there was a sharp turn to the right ahead of them.

When they shifted about and came into the room beyond, they both gasped out loud – the space was small, almost claustrophobically so, and completely barren but for a small, wooden chair, a dim lantern hanging from the ceiling, and – in the chair – an unconscious figure that looked to be about their age.

The girl had large, brown ears, short, gray hair, and white-gray fur like Harmony's, and appeared to be some kind of opossum. She was tied to the chair by her legs and arms, but did not appear to have struggled against her bonds.

Irin shook her head in disbelief. "Who could have done thi…"

"Shine!"

Completely out of nowhere, a blinding, piercing light shone in both girls' eyes from the side of the doorway, and they both wheeled about with a shocked cry.

Rubbing at their eyes hard for a long moment, the two staggered back – terrified of who might be upon them. But when Harmony finally regained her sight, she found that the figure who had cast the spell upon them from the corner of the room was still standing there – dressed in a long robe, and head tilted in confusion. "Harmony?"

"Yes?" Harmony tilted her head to the side in confusion as her vision strengthened. "How do you know my name?"

"Why, the queen told me about you, of course. And Irin too. You've made quite the impact in the palace!" the figure explained, moving forward to show the printing on his face to be that of a cheetah.

"Thanks!" Harmony giggled, almost forgetting the oddness of the situation.

"Wait… aren't you the high priest?" the dragon asked, still rubbing at her eyes.

The cheetah nodded. "Yes. My name is Illusionary. I came to search the premise for religious artifacts, as it was recently declared abandoned, but I found this opossum instead! It seems someone trapped and kept her here in this basement for a while. I'm surprised she's even alive!"

"Woah… I'm sorry we intruded… did you think we did it, is that why you flashed us?" Irin got balked, seeming nervous.

"No – but I was naturally on my guard, should the one who did still be nearby." Illusionary's tail swayed.

"What will we do to help her, now..." Harmony looked over at the poor girl again. "Can she stay at my house, maybe?"

"Hmm..." The high priest lifted a paw to his chin. "I don't see any harm in doing so. After all, I think any environment would be better and less disorientating for her than the castle or the church. And I'm sure you and your father can take care of her until she recovers, and we learn where she comes from."

Harmony purred at Illusionary's words, walking over to the opossum. "Then let's get her untied!"

Illusionary nodded, walking over to help Harmony untie the unconscious girl. But even as she concentrated on undoing the ropes, and her emotions were consumed by concern and sympathy for the opossum's wellbeing...

The voices in her head wouldn't stop.

Harmony worked diligently at the kitchen counter – stacking a cut of meat atop a rough slice of bread, and completing the sandwich with some cheese and a second slice. *She's going to love this! I hope she wakes up soon.*

Finishing the sandwich and leaving it on a plate on the kitchen table, Harmony walked back to her room and tentatively ducked inside – being careful not to make too much noise as she crept towards the opossum girl laid atop her bed.

Despite her efforts to be quiet, however, Harmony got no closer than a few feet away before the girl's eyes shot open, and she sat up urgently with a scared, disorientated look on her face.

A few moments later, she came to stare at Harmony with fear in her deep purple eyes. "Who are you? Where am I?"

"My name is Harmony Mei! And you're in my bed right now." she meowed, tail swaying slightly. "What's your name?"

"Umi Hoshi. Hoshi was my mother's name." The girl's face and head fell, seeming more sad now than scared.

"You don't have a Mom?" Harmony tilted her head with a sad gasp.

The opossum stared up at her with a blank look in response.

"S-Sorry!" Harmony spluttered a little, feeling insensitive. "I... don't have a Mom either. Just my Dad."

The opossum scoffed with surprising attitude. "Well, at least you have a Dad. I never knew mine."

That took the cat even futher back. "I'm sorry..." She bit her lip, and tried to chagne the subject. "Maybe you should follow me? I made you a sandwich."

Her attempt at bringing things back to a more positive note was successful, as the other girl stood up from the bed sharply at this, a hungry look in her eyes. "Sure."

A moment later and the two were in the kitchen, both sitting down at the table, and with the sandwich in front of Umi. It didn't remain there for long, however, before the opossum snatched it up and began to take big bites.

"You must be hungry!" the cat laughed.

"It feels like I haven't eaten since I left my last Mom...." Umi responded through a maw full of the sandwich.

"You had multiple moms?!" Harmony gasped again, leaning closer to her across the table.

Umi shrugged. "I guess. My last mom was a white moth, short and chubby. Her name was Willow. I left, though, and started to survive on my own in the castle streets. She didn't like... what I could do with my powers."

Harmony's jaw fell open, but before she could inquire further, a third voice came. "I see your new friend is awake."

The girls turned to the door to see Daku leaning on the kitchen doorway with an uneasy smile on his face.

Harmony broke out of the hug, and nodded. She was still... upset at her father for the night before, but Umi's presence was more important right now. "Her name is Umi Hoshi – I made her a sandwich."

Daku looked at the sandwich and smiled. "That's good!" He took a few steps into the room, and now met Umi's eyes. "Are you doing okay? Do you remember what happened, how you got knocked out?"

Umi shook her head. "Not quite. I was just in one of the alleys of the castle looking for food, and then someone sneaked up from behind and hit me."

"You said something about powers?" Harmony beamed, ignoring this new information.

"Yeah," the opossum answered, tone still quite mild. "I can summon different beasts and creatures... want to see?"

Daku shook his head preemtively. "Maybe not..."

But Harmony's response could not have been more different. "Yes! I want to see!" the cat girl shouted.

Umi smiled finally at her enthusiasm, and motioned with her hands toward the floor – making strange signs and motions with her fingers. Before long, a small, foot tall creature appeared on the kitchen floor – a miniature wolf made out of flames.

Daku frowned, Harmony gasped, and Umi pointed her finger at the beast with authority. "Sit!"

The wolf whined, sitting on its haunches, and looking up at Umi with pleading eyes.

Harmony gave a wide smile. "That's amazing! How do you know how to do that?"

"My first Mom – my real Mom – told me I was just born that way," Umi explained. "She could too. But then I had to... move away." Her face sobered up again. "And my other Moms didn't want to hear about it."

"This is awesome!" Harmony looked over to her father. "She has powers like me, Dad!"

"I see," he groaned, shaking his head.

"I'm still learning to control them. But what do you mean, like you?" The opossum looked intrigued.

"Learning to control them very quickly, might I add!"

Harmony and Umi turned about with a gasp, and Daku yelped out loud in shifting to see a familiar figure standing in the kitchen doorway behind them. It was the deer Kijury. The frown on Daku's face worsened.

"Kijury!" the cat girl smiled upon recovering from her initial shock.

Kijury smiled, and then walked past Daku and over to Umi to shake her hand. "Illusionary told me I'd find you here. My name is Kijury Weathers, ma'am, and I am the personal bodyguard of our queen Upholder"

Umi smiled, and returned the shake. "My name is Umi Hoshi!"

Kijury's smile deepend. "Wonderful to meet you. I couldn't help overhear you talking about your powers. And I wanted to offer to help you train and get better at using them – like I'm doing with Harmony and her dark powers. If you want to, of course!"

Harmony turned to Umi with her usual beaming enthusiasm at this. "You could train with Irin and me! It'll be fun!"

"Who's Irin?" the opossum asked, looking at Harmony now with curiosity in her eyes.

"She's my best friend! She trains with me!"

Umi looked at Kijury with a smile. "Then count me in!" she beamed, hopping out of the kitchen chair.

Kijury nodded and gestured for Umi to follow him back towards the kitchen doorway. "I'll be at the castle for a while with Umi, Harmony. Enjoy the rest of your day off!"

"Thanks, Kijury!" Harmony replied, following them out the threshold and to the sunny exterior of the house while Daku stayed inside and rested his head in his hands with an air of melancholy.

"Ready to go, Umi?" the deer asked the opossum, once they stood outside.

Umi nodded, and Harmony waved back happily. "Bye! Hope to see you soon!"

Bidding a nod and tapping the bottom of his staff on the cobblestones twice, first Kijury and then Umi began to dissipate into greenish vapor, and then vanished completely.

Even once the two had disappeared, Harmony was left smiling in the doorway. *I'm so glad we were able to save her. I'd love to have another friend. Although...*

Her face fell at the thought of the state that they had found Umi in.

Whoever did that... They're still out there. I hope the knights catch them, before something like this happens again.

8

— ● —

*F**our years later*

Time passed like a blur between training, finding a new foster home for Umi, and chores for Harmony and Irin's parents – but as it did, the three found themselves growing closer and closer to both one another and to mastery of their powers, learning new techniques and better control with each passing month.

At the beginning of one such month – right at the threshold between spring and summer – the cat woman was sleeping on the couch of the living room with her left leg and arm hung over the side, snoring loudly.

"Harmony! It's time for breakfast!" Daku called from the kitchen.

A long moment passed in silence, before he called again. "Harmony?"

Harmony's tail twitched at the sound of her name, but she didn't make to rise. "Just a few more minutes, Dad…" The cat groaned into the couch cushion.

Sighing loudly, Daku walked into the living room and over to the couch, until his shadow in the light straining through the window cast over her. He crossed his arms over the apron he was wearing. "Harmony Mei."

Harmony finally opened her eyes, looking groggily up at her father. "Oh. Morning, Dad."

"You know you have training today, don't you? You're already ten minutes late."

Her brain flared with urgency and she sat up sharply in a tangle of hair. *Oh, shit. Yesterday was the last day of the holidays that Kijury gave us.*

Her father chuckled at the cat girl's shock. "Well, I made fried toast. Come get something to eat before you leave."

Daku turned about to leave, and Harmony followed – walking behind her father into the kitchen. As she walked in, the scent of fried bread and egg filled her nose, and she gave a wide smile, sitting down at the kitchen table with an agile swing of her legs.

Her father turned back around from the stove with a plate and two pieces of toast upon it, walking over and sitting down as well.

Harmony frowned at her father. "Where's my plate?"

Daku raised an eyebrow. "You're old enough to get one yourself, Harmony."

Harmony let out a groan, but got up nonetheless – walking past her father, plucking up four pieces of bread from the plate on the counter, and putting them on her plate before settling back down with a dramatic huff.

No sooner had she done so, however, than her eyes flew open. "I forgot a fork!"

But she didn't stand up this time. She simply lifted her right paw, and a black aura began to form around it – flaring for a moment, before a fork instantly appeared in her grip.

Daku stared wide-eyed at his daughter as her paw stopped glowing, and she began to tuck in and eat. "Harmony. What did I tell you about using your powers in the house?" He frowned.

Harmony stared back, sighing, and then swallowed her current mouthful of food. "No using powers around you. Got it."

The male cat rolled his eyes, and went back to eating. Harmony did too, but not without some resentment. *He's hated my powers ever since I first began to train. And I still have no idea why.*

The two ate the rest of their meal quietly, and the next to act was Harmony – hopping up after her last bite to stand next to her chair. "I'm going to go get ready!"

"All right. Just make sure you…" Harmony disappeared in a burst of dark energy, and Daku trailed off with a deep sigh.

Appearing in her room in another dark burst, Harmony immediately hit he knee on the edge of her bed and grunted in pain. "Ow…"

But then she was moving over to her dresser and rushing about putting on the training uniform folded atop it, before teleporting back into the kitchen just as her father began to clean the table, facing away from her.

She tapped his shoulder. "Hey, Dad!"

Daku jumped, hitting his leg on the table before turning about with a startled glance. "Ow! Damn it, Harmony, I told you not to sneak up on me like that..." He sighed, and went back to wiping the table off. "I assume you're leaving now?"

"Yep! I'm meeting Irin and picking up Umi first!" she responded.

Her father folded up the towel he'd been using to wipe, and placed it over his arm. "All right. Don't be troublesome out there, Harmony. Without the queen's protection, I would have had to bail you out from the hold about ten times by now."

"Yeah, yeah... whatever, old man." She rolled her eyes, smirking.

That made Daku's scowl deepen. "Forty isn't old. You're just young."

"What are you trying to say?" Harmony squinted her eyes.

"That one day you'll be forty just like me and understand how *I* feel." her father smiled now.

Harmony stuck her tongue out. "Yeah, right!"

"Heh... now get going, you silly cat. You wouldn't want to be any more late for training." Daku chuckled.

She hugged her father, purring. Daku embraced the hug, stroking her hair. "Stay safe."

Harmony broke out and stepped back with a smile. "I will!" Dark energy swarmed around her, and she disappeared in front of his eyes.

Daku's smile faded into a frown after Harmony left. Setting the cloth onto the table, he slowly sat down at one of the chairs, cradled his head, and began to softly cry.

Harmony appeared in front of Umi's lodging house with a flutter of dark energy – smiling, and squinting about herself and at the building through the strong golden sunlight.

"Harmony?"

The cat woman turned around to see the face of her best friend, where the dragon was leaning at the outside of the lodging building. Irin was already wearing her training outfit, smiling as she looked over at Harmony.

Moving over with arms wide, the two shared a hug, and Harmony gave a wide smile of her own. "Ready to get Umi?"

"Mhm!" Irin nodded, and they separated to move through the building's front doors and look about the small but cozy lobby with its rustic paintings, and the porcupine behind the front desk.

"Hi!" Irin addressed him, waving. "Hey. Is Umi Hoshi here?"

The porcupine nodded. "She should be in her room now."

"Thank you!" Harmony and Irin beamed in unison, walking past the desk, down the hallway, and up a set of stairs until they got to the first lodging door, and came to stand in front of it.

Harmony knocked on the door. "Umi! It's Harmony and Irin!"

A few seconds passed before they heard the door unlock, and it shifted open to reveal a somewhat tired, scruffy-furred Umi Hoshi, dressed in just a shirt.

Umi smiled once she saw the two. "Hi, guys, good morning!"

"Hi!" Harmony and Irin greeted in unison, before stepping forward and following Umi into the room for a few steps before the opossum moved over to her closet and took off her shirt while looking about for her training outfit.

Irin gasped, covering her eyes. "Umi! You have guests!"

"Don't mind us." Harmony chuckled.

"Don't make me summon a water creature or something and drown you both..." Umi exhaled, before setting about putting on her training outfit. Her outfit was the same as Harmony and Irin's, but her leathers were tinted yellow.

Eventually Umi closed her closet door and looked over at the other two. "Now – are we going to head off, or not?"

"Don't be so pushy!" Harmony's eyes switched to black again with another chuckle, and she stepped up to place herself between her two friends.

"Let's go!" The cat pulled the opossum and dragon close, summoned her energy, and vanished in the span of a moment.

"Where are those three?" Kijury tapped his staff on the ground impatiently, glancing about the palace's entrance hall. He'd collected them from their houses not so long ago, but they'd appeared to have disappeared on their lunch breaks, and were already twenty minutes late for their second training session of the day.

Except that today, they wouldn't be training – he had something else in mind, and their tardiness was proving quite inconvenient already.

Just as he was about to stride off in search of them, however, Irin and Harmony rushed through the doorway and trotted over to the deer with a smile. "We're here, Kijury!"

"Ah. There you all are!" Kijury smiled, waving.

"What are we doing for the last half of the day, Kijury?" Harmony asked.

"Not sparring!" He bowed his head. "We're headed to the Guild House, where we'll get you a quest from knight Ika."

Harmony thought for a few seconds. "Maybe we'll fight a monster... or fetch a dangerous artifact!"

Kijury shook his head, unusually sincere. "Not quite. The knights have been struggling to track down a missing girl for some time, and I feel like this would be a good time for you girls to use your skills – and your minds – to work as part of the team."

The girls' jaws dropped, but the deer wasn't wasting time – moving over to them, he tapped his staff on the ground, and vanished with them in tow.

Kijury appeared with his apprentices in a well-lit room. "Welcome to the Penlight Guild House, you three!" He smiled, looking at them.

"Woah..." Umi muttered under her breath, looking around her. The guild house's walls were made of a rich, ornate wood, as were the floors, and the furniture about them was eclectic and cluttered, but still very elegant in design overall.

"Hey, guys!" a voice called from next to them.

The four turned to see a long, blonde-haired woman with a large black hat and simple black leathers waving from over near a full bookshelf.

"Hello, Ika!" Kijury greeted her, with Harmony and Umi also waving to the knight.

"Hi there!" The electric knight smiled, approaching. "I assume you're all here for the task we were supposed to pass on, so I'll get right to it." She tented one hand on her hip, and her expression became a little more sincere. "There's a child that went missing a few days ago. She's a white rabbit named Autumn. The mother said she was last with her on the path past the residential districts of the castle. And then... she simply vanished."

"A mother losing her child..." the deer man mumbled to himself, before looking over at his apprentices. "Do you three feel like you can lend a hand in the search?"

Irin was the first to respond – bearing a beaming smile while Harmony and Umi also nodded. "Mhm! We'll find her!"

Ika gave a wide smile. "That's what I love to hear! I suggest you start by the castle path – the rest of the knights have been searching parts of the city for almost a week now. There's just the manor quarter that we haven't covered yet."

Harmony nodded, and stepped back in preparation to head off.

"Good luck, future knights!" Kijury smiled.

"Thanks, Kijury!" The women replied in unison.

Harmony's body buzzed with energy, she pulled Irin and Umi close, and within moments was disappearing into thin air.

9

—— · ——

Appearing in a burst of darkness on the street outside of the guild house, Harmony, Irin, and Umi arranged themselves in a loose formation and began to make down the shop- and building-surrounded path from the castle and out towards the villages.

"I hope Autumn is okay…" Umi muttered, looking around as though hoping to note a clue or some other sign.

Harmony blinked in the brightness of the day a little, and narrowly dodged a loose cobblestone in her momentary blindness at the sudden change in light from the guild house's interior. "I'm sure she's fine. Maybe she ran away from home?"

"I *hope* that's the case." Umi shook her head as they walked. "But I have the feeling that we wouldn't have been sent to investigate if this wasn't at least a little more serious. Not serious enough to warrant the knights handling every step, but… still."

They walked for a few minutes further in silence – progressing down the path from the castle, and into the manor quarter. *Don't worry, Autumn! We'll find you and bring you home safely!*

When they reached a particularly densely packed section of the quarter, and found themselves completely surrounded by large structures with ornate fronts, Harmony glanced about them, and gestured to the left and right with both her hands. "Let's spread out."

The other two girls nodded and followed her directions, leaving Harmony on her own for a while to comb through the wandering streets to the east – occasionally brushing past denizens as she did so.

This continued for some time – almost an hour, or so it felt – until the cat girl eventually looped back to her starting point, and caught sight of Irin in a nearby alley. Moving over with a wave, she raised her eyebrows in question. "Nothing so far?"

Irin shook her head. "Nothing. But Umi said she wanted to investigate the same manor where we found her – it's still abandoned."

Harmony's brow fell, and she grumbled a little under her breath in frustration. *I hoped they were having better luck.*

Just as she was about to turn about and continue down the way with Irin in tow, however, her vision flicked to the side, and she spotted a dark, slim figure darting down a narrow alley to her right – visible to be wearing a dark cloak.

Irin's head jolted in the direction of the figure too. "Who is that?"

Harmony felt her arms surge with dark power. "I don't know, but I'm going to find out!" she growled, and darted into a run.

The figure moved at an impossibly high speed, but Harmony was close in chase – ignoring the strain and fatigue on her own body altogether. *If this is the one who took Autumn... or if they can lead me to her... The coincidence is too great.*

The figure turned a corner, and Harmony growled in frustration. "Get back here!"

But then, after rounding a corner, she skidded to a halt – seeing a sharp T section in front of her, and no sign of the figure whatsoever.

Coming up from behind with the noise of heavy panting and rushed footsteps, Irin reached after her friend with an urgently beckoning hand. "Harmony, slow down! Where did they go?"

Harmony sighed, trying to catch her own breath. "They're too fast... I couldn't get them."

"That's okay, Harmony – I'm sure they'll turn up again. But right now we have to find Umi again – I have no idea where she went, but she did say something about the manor where we found her!" Irin exclaimed.

"Let's try there, then." Harmony nodded.

Irin nodded, grabbing onto the sullen Harmony and leading her back through the alleys until they were able to latch onto familiarity and find their way to the abandoned, dusty manor just adjacent from the main street.

Once they came to the front door, the two found it open. "Don't tell me she went in already..." Harmony sighed.

Irin shrugged. "Probably!"

The two moved inside through the open threshold. The main room was well lit by the sunlight coming in through the windows, but the two recognized and moved over to the door leading to the basement instantly – with Harmony getting flashbacks from when they found Umi. *I hate it here...*

The two ran down the stairs, seeing the light on, and by the time they arrived at the base, they turned to see Umi on her knees just inside, crying.

The opossum shifted as they entered, eyes wet and red. "We were too late..." Umi whispered quietly, between sobs.

They looked up from Umi, seeing a white rabbit tied to a chair in the same place where Umi had been, those years ago. But unlike Umi, there was no question whether she was still alive. Blood was everywhere – the girl's neck was slit open, and her clothes were stained and ripped.

Harmony's eyes widened as she put a paw over her mouth, and Irin gasped, not knowing how to react to the situation. Their stomachs were lead, their limbs began to shake, and their brains struggled to form cohesive thought.

"Umi, I..." the cat woman whispered, walking over to the opossum and couching next to her to pull her in for comfort.

"I'll go tell Kijury and Ika! Stay here with Umi!" Irin spoke, voice distraught and urgent, and already turning back towards the stairs.

Harmony nodded, eyes closed and daring not to look up at the scene before them again. "Alright..."

In the long moments that followed, the cat girl ran her fingers through Umi's hair, and the opossum pressed her head into Harmony's chest.

"Harmony..." Umi whispered from the cat's chest. "Promise me if we find who did this... you won't hold back on them."

The cat hesitated in her stroking for a few seconds, before resuming and nodding her head. "I won't. I... promise." *Whoever you are... whoever did this... I'll end you.*

"Thank you, Harmony..." Umi breathed deeply, and relaxed somewhat in Harmony's embrace.

Thank you, Harmony. For Nothing.

Tension and fear shot through Harmony's body, forcing her to breathe hard to keep her nerves in check. *How? How are you back? I got rid of you so long ago!*

Rid of us? Harmony... there's only one way you'll ever do that.

She felt energy welling up within her – partially anger and shock at the foreign, threatening presence. *I'll get rid of you for good.*

At that moment, however, there came a fresh set of footsteps from the basement stairs. Harmony wheeled about to see the faces of Irin, Kijury and Ika, appearing with concerned expressions upon their faces.

The moment he stepped into the room, the deer put a hand over his mouth before he could gasp. "Ophin have mercy on her soul..."

After a long, shocked moment of silence, Ika walked over to Harmony and Umi. "Irin said you were chasing someone. Perhaps the one that did this."

Harmony sighed, shaking her head. "They were too fast for me. I couldn't keep up."

The woman nodded, placing a hand on Harmony's shoulder as Kijury moved forward to examine the body, and Umi slowly stood and wiped the tears from her eyes. "It's all right, Harmony."

Irin walked over to Harmony and Umi, pulling them into a hug – with the opossum finally managing to stop crying.

Shaking his head, Kijury frowned. "This is... unacceptable. Something the Kingdom hasn't heard of for so many years."

The deer looked over at the electric knight stood to his side. "I'd like you to notify Autumn's mother. Try not to be... *Too* forward about it."

"As you say, sir." Ika's body and saddened face glowed yellow before she dispersed into electricity.

"What do we do now, Kijury?" Irin asked.

"You three may take time to yourselves. I would understand if you'd simply wish to go home after... this." Kijury replied solemnly.

"Thanks, Kijury," the women responded in unison.

But although Harmony's tone was thankful, and her attitude still relatively chipper as usual, her thoughts were dark, and her head swimming with Umi's plea.

I'll get you next time. And end you.

Later that evening, the trio arrived at the Penlight Castle at Umi's request – winding through the largely empty halls of the palace, and out onto the all-too-familiar training yard just as the afternoon sun began to burn orange.

Once they stood in the center of the yard, Umi moved her hair to the back of her head, and tied it into a ponytail with a hairband from her pocket. "We're fighting."

Harmony's eyes widened. "You want to fight *now*?"

Umi finished tying up her hair. "After what we saw..." The opossum shook her head. "We need to be strong. To stop something like that from happening again."

The cat's jaw fell open to respond cautiously, but then she shut it again. Umi, too, had very nearly met an end like that. And how shaking the incident seemed to have been for her made a lot more sense, now.

Harmony looked over to Irin standing next to her, and gestured to the side of the training field. "I want to try something out – Irin, you should probably move!"

Irin raised her eyebrows and chuckled, before complying. "If you say so!"

When Irin was standing all the way back against the stone balustrade at the edge of the yard, Harmon turned back about to see that Umi too had retreated a little, and that she already had her hands ready to perform signs, as she always did when using her powers.

Breathing deeply, Harmony concentrated on summing her own energy, and closed her eyes for a moment. *She's right. We have to be strong. Stronger than ever before.*

But then a great roar came, and her eyes shot open in shock to see an at least ten foot tall, blue-scaled wyvern now stood in the space between herself in Umi – eyes fiery and trained right down on her.

Harmony's jaw dropped. *Damn it, Umi!*

The wyvern spread its wings, flying up into the air with a sharp jolt – keeping its eyes on her the entire time, and wasting no time in swelling out its throat and letting out a large, flickering ball of blue fire.

"Your dragon sure is wild!" the cat flicked her right paw, causing the blue flames to turn black. "Got you!" She giggled, flicking her paw again, sending the now dark ball of flames directly back where it had come from.

The flames struck and rolled over the wyvern, and it staggered back mid-air at the force of the blow – roaring out in pain, and slowly lowering to the ground until it landed completely and sat there panting and weakened.

Eventually, with a grunt of frustration, Umi waved her hands and the wyvern disappeared. Teleporting behind the opossum, Harmony hugged her. "Did I win?"

The opossum reciprocated the hug. "Yes, but you could've been gentler with Elderex."

"Yeah, yeah..." Harmony looked over at Irin. "You okay over there?"

Irin stood up, nodding. "Yeah! That fight was exciting! I want to fight Elderex, too!"

"Later," the opossum answered. "He'll have to rest up for a few hours before he's ready to summon again."

"And in the meantime, we can rest up at your place." Harmony smirked.

"It's been a while since our last sleepover. This'll be fun!" Irin exclaimed.

"Take us back to my foster mom's apartment, please," Umi asked Harmony politely.

The cat nodded eagerly – body crackling with dark energy, and already reaching out to bring the two close for the second time that day. "On it!"

The walls of the queen's bedchambers were papered ornately – almost as ornate as the wooden bed in the corner, and the dresser beneath the window. Sat just shy of that dresser with her hands folded in her lap and her head turned towards its mirror, the queen herself sighed deeply.

Behind her stood Kijury – arms also folded, and face equally concerned.

The deer bowed his head. "I.. just don't know what to do."

Upholder raised one hand. "It was inevitable, this I knew. We've been... playing thin lines for too long. The knights already all knew. There was no hiding it forever."

She turned to look up at him – eyes soft but frightened. "But now that the public knows..."

Kijury at first looked frightened too, but then something steeled in his gaze, and he nodded sharply. "We can finally put an end to this."

The queen looked a little shocked – but Kijury didn't give her time to interject. "You worry, worry, and worry. But now we can be free of this. And not live in shame any longer."

He dropped to one knee, and took her hand. "I want that. And I know you do too."

Upholder frowned lightly, and sighed once more. "I worry because I have to. About what people could think. About the child, too, for years, now." She looked up at the mirror – gazing into the faint fire that lingered in the pupils of her eyes. "But Harmony... I hope that before long I can worry a little less about her. That she can take care of herself, one day. And when it comes to us..."

She glanced back to her lover. "I suppose you're right. I think I know a solution for that, too."

Kijury stood sharply, looking over at the hound woman in confusion. "How so?"

Upholder smiled, and first stood, then knelt. "Kijury. We've loved one another for so many years, now. You've protected me and the people of our kingdom for just as long. You spend every day and every night with me. There is only one logical end to this. One right end."

Her paws clasped both of his. "Kijury Weathers. Will you marry me?"

For a long, long moment the deer didn't react, but then his expression shock wide, and he tugged Upholder up to her feet and into as tight of an embrace as he could manage. "Yes! I *will*!"

Upholder embraced the hug, kissing the deer's cheek again and again and again, before moving over to his lips.

After some time, she broke out of the kiss, and stared across at him with nothing but pure adoration in her eyes. "I love you."

"I love you too."

As she was completely unprepared for a sleepover, Harmony asked whether she could take something to wear from Umi's closet, and was able to find a set of red pajamas while the other two girls sat themselves on Umi's bed and began to eat from a bag of sweet rolls they'd bought along the way back. Umi's foster mother – a equine of some sort – lived in the apartment next to them, but Umi had been living on her own since she'd turned 18.

After Harmony stepped back into the room with 'her' pajamas on, Umi had a sweetroll in her hand, and took a bite before smirking up at the cat girl. "If you're gonna sleep in my bed again, please don't snore."

Harmon rolled her eyes. "I don't snore..."

"Again?" Irin's mouth dropped open, cutting Harmony off.

The cat chuckled nervously while sitting down next to them on the bed. "Don't worry about that, Irin."

"Hmm, okay..." Irin responded, eating the rest of her bun and forgetting about what the two said.

You can't ignore us forever, Harmony. And the cost will only grow, while you do.

A jolt of sharp pain ran through Harmony's skull with the return of the voice, causing her to shoot her hand to her head for a brief moment to press against the discomfort. *You could've stopped the one who killed Autumn. You know that, don't you? All you had to do was unleash your full power. Just once. Just to start. To take control.*

Umi noted the gesture with a concerned frown, pausing mid-bite into her bun. "Something wrong?"

Harmony shook her head hastily. "Nope! Just a bit tired."

The other girl nodded. "Alright, just let me finish and we'll get some rest."

The opossum went back to eating, and Harmony smiled. "Perfect!"

These voices... I'll ignore them for as long as I need to. Til they're gone for good.

10

The night was peaceful and free of disturbance – aside from, of course, occasional snoring from one of the three girls and limb collisions.

This calm was shattered all too soon, however, when Harmony was woken by a knock at the apartment door – one eye blinking open, and slowly untangling herself from Umi to sit up and ponder. *Who the hell is here so early?*

"Ugh..." the cat yawned, stretching and gently getting off the bed in an attempt to not wake Umi before making over to the door in the opossum's grey sweatpants.

Her paw moved towards the doorknob, but an almost tangible force stopped it just short. *Don't open that door. Act like you're not there.*

Harmony's head was pounding, now. She breathed, ignoring the voice and trying to block out the pain, and put her paw on the doorknob.

Did you not hear us? Don't open that door.

She stared forwards, confused and agitated. *You don't know who's behind the door... why do I have to listen to you?*

Harmony turned the knob defiantly, and wrenched open the door at speed – finding herself immediately face to face with a familiar robed cheetah.

"Hello, Harmony!" Illusionary greeted her with a smile. "It's been some time since we've seen one another. How are you on this blessed morning?"

She stifled a yawn with her hand in an attempt to be polite. Illusionary was a semi-common visitor to the castle, but most of the time seemed preoccupied with his business with the church. "I'm fine. I just woke up. How about you?"

He raised his chin cheerfully. "Better than ever! But this isn't just a social visit, I promise. I'm here to invite you, Irin, and Umi to a celebration at the palace hall!"

Harmony tilted her head. "A celebration? What for?"

"Why, a celebration for Upholder and Kijury's marriage!" Illusionary exclaimed.

Eyes widening, the cat woman gasped. "They're getting married?!"

She'd seen the two together, of course, and had understood that they were a pair of some sort amidst their years of training with Kijury, but that they'd do something so official, so unexpectedly... was a shock, though a brilliant one.

Illusionary nodded. "Indeed. Their relationship has made it to the criers, and before the public start whipping up scandal, they decided to make things official."

There was a sharp shuffle of movement, and Harmony turned to see both Umi and Irin standing behind her with sleepy but excited expressions on their faces.

"M'lady and Kijury?!" Irin grinned. "That's wonderful! Can we really come to the party?"

The cheetah nodded. "This will be wonderful, then! I can't wait to see you three there!" He reached down to shake Harmony's hand, and she returned the gesture firmly, which caused Illusionary's smile to widen. "So bold. Just like your mother."

A moment later he was turning about and moving away from the door to vanish back amidst the corridor outside. "Have a blessed morning!"

Harmony closed the door slowly, staring at it while thinking to herself. *My... mother.*

Umi approached from behind, tapping her shoulder. "Hello? Ophin to Harmony!" She chuckled.

Harmony shook her head free of confusion, looking back at Umi. "Hm? What do you want?"

"My sweatpants, you silly cat!" Umi answered with a sigh.

"What? They're mine now! I didn't *have* any pants to begin with!" Harmony smirked, and her tail lashed.

The opossum woman poked the cat's nose. "Fine. But just make sure you give them back, okay?"

Harmony stayed smirking. "I'll try. Did you two sleep well?"

Irin nodded. "Mhm! I sleep like a baby when you two are around!"

"You didn't snore for once, so I slept peacefully as well." Umi smirked too. "But since we've accepted an invitation, I think it's time we work out what we're going to wear to this party. We can't go in our training uniforms!"

Harmony's eyes widened, and she stepped through the apartment over to Umi's closet. "Let's take a look, then!"

A few seconds later and they were all standing before the open closet rummaging about – occasional darting off to the bathroom to put on a piece of clothing, before taking them off one after the other with incessant giggling at how silly they'd looked, most of the time.

Eventually, however, Irin emerged in an orange, thigh-slit dress that was surprisingly noble for Umi's humble collection, and Harmony's eyes widened. "Woah, you look amazing!"

Irin smiled widely. "T-thanks... Should I wear this to the party?" Irin slowly turned her body around to show how the dress looked on her.

Harmony nodded. "Suits you great, despite the fact that you and Umi are such different heights!"

Irin squinted at Harmony. "Are you calling me short?"

The cat cackled, not answering the question, but Umi only rolled her eyes. "Come on, old lady. Let's see if we can find something that even fits you."

Harmony's jaw fell for a moment, before she gave the opossum a playful shove, and the three of them got back to refining their outfits after another round of powerful giggles.

The palace hall was such a familiar place to the three of them, but just like the castle during the festival, it looked so different when decked in decorations and filled with so many people. The courtyard and the entrance hall to the throne room were absolutely packed, and there were wooden tables lined up along the walls, laden with food and drinks from the castle outside.

Standing near one of the tables with a sweet bun in hand, Harmony took a bite and looked over at her two friends standing close to her – dressed just as fabulously as they were, in her own slim, black dress. "So glad I get to go to this with you guys."

Irin nodded and took a sip from her glass, tail swaying. "It's nice to be here for something other than training. And I have to admit, those two look excellent." She pointed over to where Upholder and Kijury stood with arms linked in the center of the room, near the queen's throne.

The Queen was wearing a long, sleek black dress of her own to compliment her golden fur, and Kijury was dressed in something other than his rugged cloaks for the first time that they had ever seen – instead donning a respectable jacket as he chatted with guests.

But then Harmony frowned. *I need to talk to Upholder about what Illusionary said. About my mother.* She turned back to her friends. "Let's go talk to Upholder and Kijury."

Umi and Irin nodded, and the three women moved over to the pair just as the noble that Kijury had been talking to moved away – allowing both the deer and Upholder to greet them with a wide smile.

Kijury detatched from Upholder's side and smiled at them. "Hello, you three! Welcome to the party, and thanks for coming on such short notice!"

"Congratulations on the engagement!" Harmony nodded to both politely, and did a little swish in her dress. "And don't worry, we had plenty of time to prepare! Illusionary told us pretty early in the morning."

That caused Upholder frown unexpectedly. "Where is that priest? He said he wanted to give a speech?"

Before anyone could answer, however, there came a loud, piercing shriek from over the head of the crowd – and everyone shifted about with a gasp to see a cream-furred female cat in a long white dress dashing about with panic in her eyes, yelling out loud. "Has anyone seen her?! Tell me she's here somewhere…"

"Who?" Standing from her throne with a rush and speaking out loud in a commanding voice, Upholder walked up to the panicked cat.

"My daughter, Isabella!" the lady exclaimed with tears beginning to streak down her white cheeks. "I saw someone snatch her up, when she was playing in the courtyard… and now she's missing!"

"What does your daughter look like?" Kijury asked, tone urgent.

"She looks like me – has a pink dress on!" The lady wailed, still beyond herself with panic.

Upholder and Kijury turned around, their arms still locked with each other. "Mystic. Get Mase and Ika and go search the area for Isabella."

"On it." Mystic ran off to find the two knights.

"You three search as well," Kijury ordered Harmony and her friends.

The three women nodded in response – wasting no time in turning about and dashing off through the throne room's doors in Mystic's wake.

11

—— • ——

A few moments later, Irin, Umi, and Harmony stood outside the church – glancing to and fro in the evening light as though hoping to catch a sight of the missing cat. The entire situation was eerily familiar – except, of course, for their elegant attire.

"Well, this is a wonderful start to the night," Umi exhaled.

"Don't worry, Umi!" Irin tried to stay positive. "We'll find Isabella! But should we split up?"

"We'll cover more ground that way, just like last time," Umi replied, before looking over at Harmony. "Agreed, Harmony?"

Harmony nodded, although a little worriedly. *Just like last time... saying it like that makes me frightened we'll have the same results.* "Sure, yeah."

"I'll check near the Inn!" Irin ran off in one direction, leaving the other two girls standing alone.

"I'll check the Guild House." Umi hugged Harmony, and gave her a kiss on the cheek. "If this ends up being that person who killed Autumn... remember what I told you, okay?"

Harmony stared at the opossum for a long, thoughtful moment before nodding. "I... understand. Stay safe, okay?"

"I will." Umi broke the hug with Harmony, before turning about and making arcane signs with her hands – summoning a small ethereal wolf, who followed after her as she turned to walk away and wave over her shoulder in Harmony's direction.

Harmony breathed out and began to pace off through the streets – though not toward any location in particular. *Where to even start looking? The city is massive, as is the kingdom. The odds of finding her quickly are slim, and if this is like how Autumn went missing...*

Passing by a narrow alley, Harmony heard the snap of a twig nearby, and looked to her left to see a hooded figure standing at the end of the way just in front of her. Déjà vu flashed through her, and her eyes shot wide.

"Hey!" Springing immediately into action, Harmony darted down the alley towards the figure, arms outstretched, and welling up her powers to teleport if need be. Yet by the time she got about halfway down the alley, the figure simply... disappeared. It didn't leap out of the way, didn't duck back, it simply vanished.

Skidding to a halt at the end of the alley, Harmony glanced to and fro, breath heaving in exertion. *Where did they go?*

Get away from here! A voice echoed in her head.

"Shut the hell up... I'm getting them and killing them, this time! Just like Umi wanted." She hissed.

But as she spoke to herself, she noted a brush of movement from behind her. Harmony turned to look, but before she could completely shift about, something slammed into her head. The energy about her dissipated, her eyes went blank, and slowly she fell to the ground – utterly unconcisious.

"Wake up, dear. Can't have you missing out."

The voice was... familiar, somehow, and that triggering recognition was enough to cause Harmony's eyes to flicker open for a moment.

The pain that came afterwards forced her to clench them back shut, however – blinding, stiff, and all throughout her body. She tried moving from the position on her back she found herself, but her limbs felt after too weak and tired – leaving her to blink groggily and try to force herself to squint up into the light hanging above.

Then something loomed over her, covering the light. Harmony growled. "Get away from me..."

"I don't think that'll happen. Not after all this time." The figure sounded male.

A few seconds of blinking later, Harmony's brain started to surge with panic, and – somehow even more terrifying – recognition. Finally managing to keep her eyes open, the cat woman was able to make out the black cloaked form of the figure standing next to her, as well as the lamp hanging above her, the stone walls beyond, and the wooden platform beneath her. "Wait... there's no way..."

The figure raised their paw to the cloth covering their face, pulling it down to reveal the short, smirking muzzle of a cheetah.

"Illusionary!" Harmony could not believe her eyes.

With one sharp movement the cheetah took off his cloak altogether – throwing it to the floor with a smile, and leaving him in his usual robes. "Hello, my sweet Harmony."

Unable to believe her eyes, Harmony stammered. "W-where's Isabella?"

Illusionary shook his head. "She's of no use, now. A means to an end. But you..." He began to approach the platform where Harmony was laying, powerless.

Harmony panicked, yelling. "Get away from me! You're... sick!"

But then he covered her mouth, and leaned down to kiss her neck. Once more she struggled to move, but her body remained too weak. *The second I can move... I'll kill him! I'll shred him!*

Eventually he lifted his paw, and stepped back. "You know why I use this manor? It was in my father's family, long ago. Long before they dishonored themselves, just like my father did himself again." The priest shook his head. "Not that anyone will ever trace it to me. To who I used to be. It's my perfect refuge, for now. The knights can't even find a single missing girl, and you know what?"

He smiled, more gloating and cruel than ever. "I think they'll never find you, either."

"You damn monster... I'll kill you..." She tried to move again, to no success.

"Not if I silence your little screeching first! Time for another dose, I think." Illusionary chuckled, reaching down to pull a vial from the pocket of his robes.

Harmony stared at the bottle, and her eyes widened in dark, sickening realization. "My medicine…" she muttered. *So that's why I can't move or use my powers.*

"Correct!" Illusionary responded, uncorking the bottle. "Yes, it does help suppress the curse – I didn't want things going awry before the time was right, after all – but that's not its only use."

Moving over to her again, Illusionary roughly grabbed the back of Harmony's head and tilted the vial to her lips – not stopping when refused to swallow it down, and continuing to pour until the flood of liquid almost threatened to drown her.

Next, tossing the vial off to the side with a shattering crash, the cheetah chuckled and reached down to begin tearing at the waist of Harmony's dress. "And might I say… you look beautiful! Those lips… that dress… your heels!"

"Don't touch me…" Finding it harder to move by the moment, Harmony teared up, doing her best to hold back sobs.

"I'll touch you all I want." He stroked a paw through her hair while his other continued to work. "My sweet plaything."

He gave a harsh rip at the top of her dress. "Doesn't this feel lovely?" He leered, rubbing at her breasts. She didn't respond, looking away from him, and in response Illusionary stopped rubbing and forced her to look at him with both paws. "Obey me, or your precious friends Irin and Umi will be next. Now, doesn't this feel *lovely*?"

Harmony nodded against her will, swallowing the violent disgust and anger welling up within her.

"Good!" Illusionary kissed her on the cheek, as though sealing the deal. "You know, I'm tuly so glad to have you here. I couldn't have your mother. Daku was always, always in the way – oh how I prayed to Ophin that he would drink himself to death, but no. Yet now, at least, I have the next best thing. Or, perhaps, something even better… even fresher…"

His hand trailed down to the side of her dress almost tenderly, before tightening and giving another harsh rip that split it all the way down the middle – leaving her exposed beneath both his body and gaze. "Better than Autumn, or, for that matter, your precious friend Umi."

She hissed as loudly as she could, though it waved and spluttered in fear. "I'll kill you, Illusionary..."

One last shift of cloth – this time from the cheetah's own clothing – and sinister chuckle. "Good luck, you adorable thing!"

Soon, he began. And all the while, Harmony kept her eyes locked on the lantern hanging above them – trying as hard as she could to blank him and everything out utterly. Everything, at least, except the rage. *I'll kill him! I'll rip his heart out!*

The second I'm free, I'll end this man.

The search for Isabella continued fruitlessly as the evening wore on and on – and eventually Irin, Umi, Mystic, Ika and Mase ended up back outside the palace's courtyard. Most of the guests had gone home by now, although there were a few stragglers, and a few other guests inside where Upholder and Kijury were still questioning Isabelle's mother.

"Did you find any sign of her?" Mystic questioned the younger two.

The opossum sighed heavily. "My wolf couldn't catch a scent. No hints at all so far."

Looking around with a frown, Irin turned back to the others in question. "Where's Harmony?"

"I thought she was with you two," the fire knight responded with a frown.

Worried, Umi spoke. "Nope... we should find her, it's getting late."

Irin thought to herself, putting a claw on her chin. *If I was Harmony, and was searching for a missing child... where would I go first?*

"Uh... Irin?" Mystic tapped Irin's shoulder.

"The manor!" Irin blurted it out in an instant.

Confused, the electric knight tilted her head. "Manor? Which manor?"

But the dragon girl was already dashing away town the path, with a wide-eyed Umi just behind her.

"Hold on!" Mystic sprinted after the two, with Ika in tow.

Mase sighed, walking after as well. "This is fun."

When it was over, Illusionary pushed back from her with a sick, satisfied sigh, and picked up some of his clothes. "I wish I could keep you alive for longer! You're a keeper!"

Harmony moved her head to the side, watching Illusionary as he redressed partially and moved over to his cloaks in the corner of the room – retrieving a long, cruel knife from within the folds.

Turning back to her, he smiled cruelly. "But, well... We can't have everything. The best things can only be enjoyed once. And now is your time to make peace with Ophin, my dear."

The girl tensed her limbs harder than ever before in an attempt to move something – anything – to defend herself. "You think you'll get away with this?"

"I always do!" He shook his head slowly as he approached. "Because what I do is Ophin's will, and I am his servant. I need not answer for my necessary deeds."

He was within arm's reach, now – lining up his knife with her neck oh-so carefully. At that precise moment, however, there was a burst of pressure in her skull, and the voices in her head began to scream and chatter. *Kill him! Take his life!*

Harmony flinched hard – hands flying to cradle her skull, and expression curling up in first pain and then shock as she realized that she had moved. Illusionary too was stunned at the sudden change and stepped back – giving the cat girl jus enough time to collect herself and roll off the opposite side of the platform to him.

A second later she was facing her assaulter with a growl. "Illusionary."

Eyes flaring with a little fear of his own, now, the cheetah hefted his knife, but Harmony soon flicked her hand and sent out a burst of dark energy to fling it off to the side before dashing in at speed with both fists outstretched.

Panicking at the advance, Illusionary's paws glowed with a white aura, and he flashed his powers in her eyes just as he had when they had discovered Umi. "Shine!"

But Harmony had her eyes closed – and the next thing she felt was her hand impacting in, shattering, and then piercing through Illusionary's chest. Roaring out loud, she raised her head in anger. "Go to hell, you failed priest!"

By the time she opened her eyes, the cheetah man was gasping for air and looking down at his chest in disbelief – where a bloody mess was spreading out around Harmony's arm.

Slowly, painfully, he glanced up to meet Harmony's eyes one last time, before he slumped, and the light left him altogether.

All that was left was silence. Withdrawing her hand slowly, Harmony allowed the priest's body to slump to the floor, and found his crushed, gory heart clutched within her hand.

The sight of the blood, the thought of what had happened... What Illusionary had done to her and all those girls...

Harmony could hold back the tears for not a second longer.

At that exact moment, adrenaline still running through her veins, Harmony heard urgent footsteps coming down the stairs towards her. No sooner had she wheeled about than she saw Umi dashing down the base and into the room – eyes wide as soon as she saw what lay before her, and soon to be followed after by Irin, Mystic, and Ika, who were equally astonished.

The cat woman smiled up at Umi, tears dripping onto the floor. "It was him, Umi..." she whimpered, letting Illusionary's heart drop from her hand with a dull, final thud.

"Oh, Harmony..." Umi ran over to her and pulled her into a hug with absolutely no regard for the blood across her front – only to be joined seconds later by Irin.

Harmony smiled bittersweetly and embraced the hug with her friends, crying with them.

Eventually when they broke apart, Mystic came over with wide, panicked eyes. "Can you explain what happened here, Harmony?"

She took a deep, shaky breath. "Illusionary is the one who killed Autumn. And Isabella, too... I don't know where Isabella's body is."

Ika chimed in next, glancing down concernedly at the state of Harmony's dress. "And what... did he do to you?"

That made Harmony's head sink down to glare at the floor, and her heart stop for a moment. *Don't think about it. Don't think about it for now.* "He gave me the medicine that I've taken since I was a kid, to control my magic... and I lost control of them altogether. I couldn't move. Then he took off my clothes and..."

She couldn't speak anymore. At least, not to say that. So instead she stuttered out something else. "He killed them. He killed them all."

Nobody said anything for a long, tense, tearful moment. And then everyone present converged upon Harmony – Irin, Umi, Mystic, and even Ika. Illusionary's body was forgotten, and all that mattered was the poor, beaten cat.

Through all these voices... I can hear him still.

The Queen and Kijury – their celebrations called off the second the news had reached them -were beyond shocked when the girls, Mystic, and Ika arrived. Kijury could not speak but for horror, instead simply stepping forward to embrace Harmony after she had finished explaining what had happened.

Yet there was nothing to do. The deed was done. Illusionary was dead, and now the only thing to do was to clean up the mess that he had caused, and bar off his family's mansion forever – as should have been done long ago.

After some time spent talking and comforting in the castle courtyard, the Queen turned to Harmony with a serious expression and raised eyebrows. "I understand now may not be the time to ask this... but should such a thing come to pass... do you intend to care for the child?"

Still grappling with the concept and what Upholder meant, Harmony lowered her chin, took a deep breath, and nodded. "Yes. I... couldn't imagine anything else."

Not smiling, but also not frowning, Upholder nodded. "Good."

At this exact moment, however, there was a kerfuffle from the near distance, and all present turned over to the courtyard's entrance to see another feline figure rushing over – unmistakable as Harmony's father.

"Harmony Mei!" the cat exclaimed, tears falling from his eyes. He ran over to his daughter, and immediately pulled her into a hug.

Harmony returned the embrace, and over his shoulder she could see Mase and Ika rushing after with exhausted looks on their faces. "We tried to calm him down!" Ika shouted.

Daku pushed back from the hug to snarl at the knights and queen around him. "Calm down? After everything your kingdom did to my daughter? After what you did to my wife..."

Daku froze up, realizing what he said. Kijury stiffened, too, and Upholder's eyes widened.

Harmony turned to her father in confusion. "To Mom? What did they do to her?"

But Daku's face had hardened, and his eyes refused to meet hers. "Enough of this. Let's go home, Harmony."

Growling now, the cat woman's face darkened. "What did they do to her?"

"Harmony. Let's go home. Now." He ordered.

Harmony stared at her father in shock – but allowed him to take her paw and begin walking hastily towards the courtyard's exit once more with one lingering, confused glance back at her friends.

The queen exhaled, looking over at Irin and Umi. "You two may go home. It's been... a long day for all of us."

"Yes, Upholder," the two women replied.

Daku and Harmony travelled home in silence – arriving at the door to their house just as the evening sun vanished from the sky entirely.

They didn't say anything to one another while stepping inside, either – not until they were both standing in the landing, and Daku finally glanced up at his daughter with tears in his eyes. "You're home now. And you don't have to have anything to do with the kingdom ever again."

That broke Harmony's silence too – her voice dark, and determination clear. "No."

She took a step closer to her crying father.

"I've had enough. Enough playing hiding games, enough lying – I think it's time we talked."

12

— · —

Daku's eyes widened, and he took a step back. "H-harmony. After all this... don't turn on me. I just want to protect you and... look what happened."

Sighing, she rolled her eyes, and took a step forward. "This only happened because you won't tell me about my fucking mother, Dad. I need to know."

That was enough to wipe the concern and softness off his face, and to replace it with hard stubbornness – the same reflexive anger that had brought him to strike out at her that one drunken afternoon so long ago. "This isn't the time, Harmony. Tonight has been... far, far too hard, already, and... there's nothing to tell."

That brought Harmony to anger too. "There is!" she growled. With all that had happened, nothing scared her anymore. "And I'm done not having answers!"

But Daku only shook his head, face impassive but for his clear frustration. "I've raised you for twenty years. Twenty, Harmony. I've endured all of this pain for you. The kingdom, your powers... and I dealt with it, because I love you, Harmony. It is your duty to respect me in return."

Harmony stared at her father once more – feeling energy welling up within her arms, chest, and eyes. "I want to know. I want to know now. Enough waiting."

Daku's eyes steeled on hers, and slowly, insidiously, they began to tinge black – a light mist appearing about his shoulders and upper arms. "You will not make demands of me. You will go to your room, and never go to the kingdom again."

Her own eyes widened. *Dad has powers?*

But then her father was lashing out to grab Harmony's arms in an effort to pull her forward, assumedly towards her room, and the cat girl's fighting instincts snapped into action. Hissing, she twisted to the side and shoved Daku hard – sending him stumbling a little.

This only seemed to anger him further, however – as when he reeled back up, it was with a dark-fisted, arcane-infused strike that very nearly caught the side of his daughter's face. *Why is he... like this? Is he also losing control?*

"Dad, stop this!" Just barely dodging, she stepped back, and dropped into a proper fighting stance opposite her father.

Yet Daku's eyes were leaking strong streaks of dark already, and there appeared to be no reasoning with him as he lunged forward once more. "I told you to go to bed, damn it! You're so... stubborn!"

That last word was punctuated by the first in a flurry of sharp blows that forced Harmony to shift back and press her back against the door – dodging for as long as she could, and then wincing and reeling in pain as strike after strike hit her chest and chin. She didn't fight back, for now – simply unable to believe that he would do this. That he had... the darkness, too.

Between defending against strikes and trying her best to try to escape from her pinned position, Harmony saw tears streaking down from Daku's inky black eyes as he punched again and again. "Why can't you just... listen? Why couldn't she listen? Why can't you just... stay here?"

Taking a deep breath as the male cat hesitated for a moment, seeming to reel back for a final, more powerful strike, Harmony growled and yelled. And with her yell, a dark force exploded from her body – shattering and shaking some of the ornaments in the room, and shoving Daku back hard against the opposite wall and the furniture there.

The furniture, and... the extended wooden spires of the empty coat hanger just next to the cabinet. Which were now protruding from Daku's chest. Which were now coated in blood.

Harmony's brain stopped the second she registered what she was seeing. Moving slowly, almost as though the entire moment were in slow motion, she stepped forwards – watching with wide, horrified eyes as the darkness left her father's eyes and body.

Voice faint, Daku smiled over at his daughter from his limp, marionette position against the wall. "Harmony... this changes nothing. I'll always love you. Just like I loved your mother. That's why I can't... that's why I won't..."

His next words faded to nothing, the cat's eyes drifted shut, and then... his body slumped completely.

Stepping forward faster now, she shook her father's shoulder weakly, hand trembling. "Dad, get up."

He didn't respond, or move. Harmony's eyes began to shed tears of her own. *No... no...*

Slowly, she fell to her knees before her father's impaled, lifeless body, not able to think or do anything else but fall to disbelief and the adrenaline leaving her veins.

This is your fault, Harmony. A voice rang in her head.

"No! It's not! He should've answered me when he had the chance!" Head shooting up to the ceiling, Harmony yelled back out loud, her voice reverberating off the walls.

What will Irin and Umi think when they find out you're a murderer?

That broke something inside her. The thought, the words. The idea that her father was... gone forever. And worst of all, the fact that it had all been for nothing.

So she cried. And cried. On her knees, curled up on the floor – doing anything not to be brought face to face with the man who had once loved and cared for her.

Who, she realized now, likely had had so much more to him than she knew.

The morning sky was cloudless – the sun hiding just behind the rank of trees that surrounded the back of Harmony's house, and the golden gleam filtering through them turning light pink upon the flowers that filled the yard itself.

Harmony knelt in front of a single square, rough patch of dirt, with her eyes closed and her hands folded. She'd buried her father late last night, when she thought there was the least chance of anyone watching. And now… she was simply taking in the place where she had lived all her life so far one last time.

She didn't think she'd be back – not any time soon, at least.

This had been… an accident, hadn't it? One could even say that father had been at fault – he had attacked first, after all. He had chosen to put his life before her simple, torturous question.

Regardless, however, the fact remained that she had made absolutely no progress on the cause that had brought her here in the first place.

You still need your answers, Harmony.

A few minutes later, she finally rose to her feet above the patch of dirt, and let dark energy swell within her once more.

"Time to go."

Her form was consumed by dark, and she disappeared from the yard.

First, Harmony appeared in Umi's apartment room. When she appeared, she saw that the lights were dimmed, and that the opossum was sitting on her bed.

As soon as the cat appeared, however, her eyes widened, and she got up urgently to run over and give her a hug. "Harmony! What are you doing here?"

Without responding, Harmony kissed her on the lips. The opossum stood in surprise as she kissed her, but soon embraced the kiss after a few seconds.

The two remained close for a long, almost endless moment, before Harmony broke out of it with a deep, sincere look in her eyes. "I love you."

"I… love you too, but what's this about?" Umi said with a confused look.

She stepped back, shaking her head. "Don't… worry about that. I'm probably just going to do something stupid."

Umi frowned. "That doesn't explain anything – where are you…"

But then the cat woman disappeared.

Umi sighed, walking over to her bed, and sitting down on it hard.

"Stay safe, you silly cat…"

Next, Harmony appeared in Irin's room – sending out a puff of dark energy just short of her desk and mirror. The dragon, who was dressed in casual clothes and had been at her open closet doors rummaging about, jumped in surprise, and turned about to greet her friend with a bewildered but worried expression. "Harmony! What are you doing here? I was worried when I didn't hear from you last night, but I thought you might just be recovering after... what happened."

"Look." The energy disappeared from about the cat's arms and body. "This might sound crazy, but... I want to go to the castle. Upholder knows what happened to my Mom, and I'm not leaving until I get answers."

Irin stared at her best friend for a long moment before giving a wide smile. "Then I'm in! Just let me get my training outfit on."

"Huh? You're in? Why are you happy about this?" The cat looked confused, and continued to watch after in surprise as the dragon girl plucked her training uniform out of the closet before her.

Irin tsked, finally pulling back and beginning to put the uniform on. "You're my best friend, Harmony! I'll do anything I can to help you, you know that."

Harmony teared up, hugging her even though she was only halfway dressed. "Irin... you're the best!"

"No, you are!" The dragon's tail thumped about behind her. But then she glanced over to the doorway at the opposite end of the room. "Hold on..."

She went over to her door, peeking her snout out. "Mom! Dad! I'm going somewhere with Harmony! I'll be back later!"

"Okay, sweetie! Have fun!" the voice of Dorthro echoed from downstairs.

Irin turned back to Harmony. "*Now*, I'm ready!"

Smiling, Harmony let her aura grow, and grabbed Irin's shoulder gently – teleporting to the castle with her.

The women appeared just outside the entrance from the courtyard into the hall of the queen's palace, and began to move forwards at a hesitant pace. It felt strange being here so late, when all the guests and guards were at rest, for the most part.

Midway down the hall, the cat looked at Irin. "You know you don't have to do this, right?"

Irin nodded. "Mhm! But I want to help you, so, that's what I'm doing!"

At first the dragon's optimism and loyalty only made Harmony smile, but then her thoughts ticked over, and she stopped where she stood, just short of the door to the throne room. "I've noticed something as the years went by, Irin."

Irin stopped next to the cat, looking over at her. "Hm?"

"Every time I got out of control with my powers, you were always there to calm me down. And to forgive me – even when we first met." Harmony took her friend's hand. "Thank you for being there for me, Irin. Especially... right now."

The dragon could only smile and hold her best friend close.

A few seconds later, the women stood in front of the door, and Harmony turned to her friend with a sincere look. "This is where I'll get my answers, Irin. We might have to fight... is that okay?"

Irin nodded, a wide smile across her face. "Yeah! I'm ready!"

She grinned gratefully at Irin's response, and then the two turned to move through into the throne room. The room was just as they remembered it, cleaned up and cleared after the engagement party, and occupied as usual by only the Queen and her soon to be husband, who was stood next to the throne talking into her ear.

"Upholder!" Harmony shouted, striding forward with purpose until she was quite near to the throne. Irin followed behind, looking a little timid now.

Upholder sighed, getting up to face Harmony. "It doesn't surprise me you're here after how you and your father left, Harmony." She watched warily as Harmony got closer. "Did Daku tell you everything?"

Harmony shook her head sharply. "No. No answers. He wouldn't give me anything, when I just... have to know."

Placing one hand on the arm of her throne and another on her head, Upholder frowned. "Then I am relieved. Daku may be stubborn and driven by fear... but he aims only for your own good, Harmony. As do I. That is why we protect you, and that is why you cannot know."

The cat girl lowered her chin in the queen's direction. "I came here to get those answers out of you. And I will, whether you're willing, or not"

"This has gone too far."

Kijury's frame stiffened and his leg moved forwards as though he intended to advance, but Upholder extended her long, thin arm in front of his chest, and shook her head. "Kijury. Let me handle this."

Mouth open and confusion evident across his face, the deer frowned. "I cannot allow them to threaten you, my queen."

Yet Upholder merely shook her head. "I mean no disrespect, but this is... a danger beyond your league, my love. Please, leave us."

The deer hesitated for a long, tense moment, but then the queen rose from her throne sharply, and he bowed for a moment before turning and making towards the door at the side of the throne chamber with only one last fearful, conflicted glance back towards the two girls standing in the center of the room.

Now standing with her head bowed, Upholder sighed. "I don't want this. I haven't protected, planned, and worried painstakingly for two decades for things to come to this, despite everything."

She raised her eyes, and in them was a flickering fire. "But Kijury is right. I cannot and will not stand by and allow you to make demands of me, as though you do not understand the gravity and the grave importance of my decisions."

Staring at Upholder and bewildered by her stubborn response, rage built up within Harmony. *Why can't you just tell me?* "You think I don't understand? Why do you think I came here like this? I know I can never... just know. You all think you're so much smarter than me and I hate it!"

That seemed to sadden the queen, rather than anger her, and her head fell again. "If you came with stubbornness and violence on your mind, then so be it."

Harmony glanced over at her best friend, sensing that this banter was not long to last. "Do you still want to do this?" She asked, hoping she'd say no.

But Irin only nodded, giving her a wide smile.

Upholder kept her stance throughout this interaction, staring darkly into Harmony's eyes.

"Your moves, Mei and Ishii."

Irin's claws, and arms, turned to stone. Harmony's paws glowed ever brighter with their misty, black aura.

And then it began.

In a flash, the cat teleported to Upholder's right, and aimed a sharp kick towards her face. At the same time, Irin charged – releasing a barrage of sharp stones from her arm. But before either of their strikes could land, the queen was simply... gone.

For a second both girls were staggered and forced to glance about in confusion as their attacks failed, but then the queen reappeared in a flash, and opened her muzzle with a sharp, powerful bark. "Halt!"

The arcane force of the word staggered Harmony further – causing both her and Irin to wheel about to face the queen again in an effort to not be caught off guard. "I know you two can do more than that." Upholder said, furrowing her brow and stretching out her long, graceful arms.

"Then I'll show you more!" Harmony roared – dashing forward towards Upholder, and flicking a powerful blast of dark energy at the Queen's sword. The blade was successfully sent flying out of her grasp and clattering to the floor, but even as Irin too closed the gap with a blow aimed at Upholder's face, she was not yet defenseless. The Queen sidestepped both girls' advance, and met the dragon's punch with a rock-hard fist strike of her own to Irin's neck.

The dragon girl staggered back quite some distance at the blow, clutching at the place where she had been struck. Standing still with her arms raised defensively, Upholder looked over at Harmony as Irin recovered. "Do you yield?"

Harmony growled at the hound. "I'll never yield."

The Queen's face fell yet further – not with anger, but with true sadness. "A mistake I thought we'd trained you better than to make, Harmony."

Then something in her steeled, and she turned to face the cat, now. "I hoped that this day would never come. I tried. Every day, my mind wrapping around every precaution and possibility to stop this from happening again."

The girl's eyes widened. *Again?*

But then there was a flurry of movement, and Upholder was suddenly in front of her – shoving her forward with a combination of strength and magic, and jamming her into one of the stone walls of the throne room with a deep, shaking impact.

"Harmony!" The dragon yelled – charging at Upholder yet again, and launching a barrage of sharp stones from her arm.

But the stones didn't even get within feet of the queen before her golden energy flung them straight back at Irin – forcing her to block with both arms and stagger a little.

In the single moment that she was unsteadied, Upholder advanced and stood over her – folding her arms elegantly to level burst after burst of energy and sharp, calculated blow after blow towards the dragon girl. Irin yelped, blocking her face with her stone claws, but Upholder saw that as no barrier – slamming into them, and causing her to wince in pain.

"Irin!" Harmony exclaimed – scrambling back to her feet, teleporting over to Upholder, and wrenching back with all her might in an effort to pull the queen away. And she succeeded, unexpectedly – sending the hound woman flying back in a tumble that she turned into a graceful flip at only the last moment before coming down on her feet hard.

"I'll kill you if you hurt her!" The cat yelled after Upholder as they both recovered, blood dripping from the edge of her cheek, and the dark energy crackling about her form brighter than ever.

The queen stood her ground for now, but Irin moved closer to her friend – panting, but apparently okay. "Harmony, you don't look so well... Maybe I should take over?"

Harmony shook her head determinedly. "I'll be okay."

But then Upholder was advancing once more – darting forward in a flash to knee Harmony in the stomach before Irin could react, and then pummeling her in the side.

She's so damn fast! The cat let out another grunt of pain as the hound slammed her fists into her ribs. *I can't react fast enough!*

Making use of a brief break in the blows, Harmony teleported away some feet across the throne room, leaving Irin to finally wheel about and raise her arms just in time to stop the queen's next merciless blow.

"Yield!" The queen roared as the dragon girl struggled to recover from this latest assault.

But Irin only shook her head and readied her arms yet again, a deeply stubborn expression spreading across her face as the artifacts of stone jutting out from her body grew longer, and her arms thicker and broader than ever before. "Never, Upholder. I won't let you hurt Harmony. I won't let anyone hurt her.

"Choose your words wiser than your friend, Irin. You may regret it." Stepping back and lowering her fists, Upholder instead folded her palms together, and began to draw forth a long, glowing sword from between them as she spoke.

"Don't you dare talk like that about her!" The dragon dashed at Upholder yet again – sharp stones slithering up her arms as she prepared a ranged attack once more. True to form, she launched the shards at the queen – sending them flying even faster than before.

Just like last time, however, the queen took no harm – standing her ground, and deflecting each projectile upon the blade of her sword with a small flare of flame. Frustrated and letting out a little roar, Irin gave up on that tactic altogether – instead hardening her fists with grey, hard energy, and rushing forward with her whole body – trying to close the gap between herself and the queen as closely as possible.

Even then, the queen had already stepped back in a defensive strike – and Harmony reached out one arm in warning and fear at the measured concentration in her eyes. "Irin, be careful!"

Yet it was too late. Irin reached her target, yes, but Upholder's sword was soon between them in a long, true strike – carving into and across Irin's middle, leaving a deep gash in her chest, and sending the dragon girl skidding across the floor with a dull, thudding tumble.

Harmony's eyes widened, and the dark energy disappeared from about her. "Irin!" she yelled, getting up and running over to Irin's form – fight forgotten and tears already beginning to stream from her eyes as she fell to kneel on the stone.

Irin shook her head, not seeming shocked or upset. "Shouldn't have... led with my head." The dragon woman coughed, and blood leaked from her lip.

"Irin, please... Not like this... Use your magic..." Harmony cried.

"Harmony... please tell my parents I'll miss them... and Umi, too! But most of all... I'll miss you." Irin smiled at her.

Harmony placed her head on Irin's chest, patting urgently as if she could possibly do anything to aid the severity of her injury, which was bleeding intensely onto the stone floor of the throne room.

"D-don't leave me!" She shook Irin's shoulders, but the dragon's smile was slowly fading, and her eyes were slowly going dull. "Irin! Irin..."

"What will you do now, Harmony?"

Harmony glanced up sharply at that – seeing the queen standing nearby with a stern but conflicted look upon her face. Yet there was no conflict within Harmony, now. Rage swelled up within her, and tears ran down from her eyes as she stood up. "You'll pay for this..."

Upholder shook her head. "You won't win."

But Harmony was no longer listening. She stood still and extended both arms – allowing a thick, dark aura to slowly cover them, all the way up her chest to her face until her muzzle itself was covered in the inky black leaking from her.

All the while, the cat girl stared at the Queen – using her anger to fuel and build her armor, until it had clad her form completely.

Upholder watched in first confusion and then horror as this transformation took place – before her brow furrowed and she moved back into a fighting stance. "I didn't think I'd see this again. This is your last warning – stand down."

Harmony snarled – voice dark and distorted. "Not until I avenge Irin. I'm going to make sure you rot six feet under."

Then she let out a roar at Upholder, charging at her like a feral animal. Her new, solid form appeared bulky and heavy, but she was moving faster than ever before –

following up with rough, brutal blow after blow between dodges from the queen, and taking each movement with a beyond supernatural level of strength.

And yet the Queen dodged every attack Harmony threw at her effortlessly. The cat girl responded by upping the her speed and ferocity, but that was just the opening that Upholder needed – grabbing Harmony's wrists, using her momentum against her, and bringing her about with a sharp lurch to slam into one of the stone walls of the throne room.

While the cat girl was disorientated, Upholder prepared her final, shattering blow – summoning every cell of fiery energy in her body, and letting it out through another powerful yell. "Halt!"

An enormous force emitted from Upholder's maw once more – crashing over Harmony, and shattering her armor into thin tendrils of black aura. Beneath them, once the force dissipated, her face was exposed – tears running in thick rivulets down her cheeks, and eyes wide with distress.

For a long moment the cat staggered on her feet, wobbling between attempts to come back to her fighting stance, and seeming close to falling to her knees. Eventually, the second option came to pass – with the cat girl thudding to the ground, and letting out a loud, heartbreaking sob. "I just wanted to know who my mother is..." she said. "I didn't want Irin to die..."

The queen bowed her head. "I didn't want my family to die either, but I overcame that."

Harmony looked up at Upholder, tears dripping onto the concrete. "W-What?"

Upholder pushed her flame-colored hair back, took a deep, steadying breath, and began to speak. "Let me tell you a story, Harmony."

"The story of how I became who I am. How I became... Upholder."

13

— · —

A long, long time ago, before I came to the city of Penlight, I used to live in a village on the kingdom's borders with my mother, father, and siblings.

A young Upholder sat at a kitchen table, waiting for something. She was kicking her legs beneath her, giggling to herself.

Life was simple as a child. No kingdom to protect. No curses to ward away.

The girl watched as a tall, golden-furred woman – her mother – levitated a full plate across the room from the kitchen counter to rest upon the table in front of her. "There you go, Destiny. Enjoy!"

"Thanks, Mom!" Destiny responded, and picked up her fork to eat.

I have told no one besides Kijury my first name in a… long, long while. Since even before I became queen. My father gave me that name. Even after all these years… I still find myself hoping that I bear it well in his honor.

Destiny's mother raised her head from stirring to call out. "Kids! Dinner is ready!"

A few moments later, two small dogs dressed in matching sweaters ran in – hopping into their seats. Following soon after was a taller, older dog in her late teens, who sat next to Destiny with a smile. *I still remember their faces. My mother, Xyla Upholder. My little siblings, Wilson, and Allison Upholder. And my older sister, Servillah Upholder.*

"Halt!" Wilson barked at Allison.

"Halt!" Allison barked back, giggling.

"I see you kids are taking after me, eh?" A bigger dog walked into the kitchen – smiling at everyone, and causing all four children to glance up.

"Dad!" Wilson and Allison said in unison.

Eldon Upholder. A dog with a fierce bark. My father. He had the strongest powers out of us all, and used them at his work at the forge in a town quite far away – so far, in fact, that we often did not see him for weeks at a time. But for now he was home, and we were happy.

Eldon sat at the table, ruffling the twins' hair. "What's for dinner tonight, Xyla?"

"Just steak and salad, dear! I used the meat you bought so it wouldn't go to waste!" Xyla replied, sitting down at the same time as using her powers to lower a plate down in front of Eldon.

Eldon chuckled. "Wonderful! And how are my children doing tonight?"

There was a flurry of answers, before the others got their food too, and began to eat eagerly amongst their chatter.

I miss those times. Where the world made sense. Where I was protected, instead of a protector. Where everything was in one piece.

But then, that evening, a thick chill set in over the land surrounding our house. And it soon turned to a storm – thunder booming right about our roof.

I didn't mind the storm, nor the rattling of the wind. I slept peacefully through most of the night – until at least, I heard something shatter loudly, and scrambled out of my bed to the threshold of my room.

Listening from the doorway, I heard yelling from the front of the house. It was an unusual amount of noise, even for a house full of loud kids, and it didn't take me long to identify the voices of unfamiliar men amongst it.

I don't know what kind of people had come to our house, or who had sent them. To this day, I still don't know. But I heard them asking questions. About our powers. About how they had learned that the people in this house had supernatural abilities

I didn't know what they meant at the time – sure, my family was able to do things without our hands, using just our minds, but that had always been what I had known, and I'd never thought that these abilities were anything out of the ordinary.

But then I heard their voices raising, and the visitors growing angry. I heard them demanding us to come with them – my parents, my siblings, all of us – and my father refusing, saying that he would rather die than become a prisoner.

And, after the pleading and reasoning faded, it wasn't long before I heard screams.

Scampering up, Destiny ran over to the doorway of the next room – peeking through the just-ajar door, and seeing... a sight she could never forget.

Three dark, cloaked figures with masks were standing in the open doorway. And my parents... their bodies were already on the floor. Or, at least, my mother's was. My father was slumped against the wall, gasping noiselessly and clutching at a stab wound through his heart.

I was too scared to move. I didn't know what to do.

Next, in a shuffle of frightened, disorientated footsteps, two smaller figures clattered out into the entry hall, and began to wail loudly. Allison and Wilson. Soon after them came Servillah, yelling at them to get back in hiding.

But before Servillah could move in front of her younger siblings... the cloaked men struck.

Moving like syncronised clockwork, they moved forwards to the disorientated younglings and stabbed cleanly – a single strike to each child's throat, and then a long, curving cut at dashing Servillah as she came into the center of the room.

I watched all three of them die in front of my eyes.

I wanted to rush out. I wanted to scream and cry, to wail at the feet of those who had done such terrible things. But instead I simply froze in the doorway of the darkened room, until the men were satisfied my family was dead and finally left.

The tears felt endless. I never thought I'd stop crying. That night, still and numb, I wished I could join my family in heaven.

And when the morning came, I couldn't bear to stay in the house, with bodies I couldn't bury and memories that brought me to cry at even thought. Or to go to any of the nearby homesteads, in fear that the men would be there too, or that I would be turned in. So I lived in the forest for a long time – surviving off the leaves and berries I found in bushes.

One day quite like any other, however, I heard shouting and fighting while amidst my daily foraging. I ducked behind some trees near the clearing where the noise was coming from, and saw two tall, cloaked men with weapons drawn.

And before them... was a boy. Bleeding from his side, holding a crimson-stained cloth to his face, and on his knees. Something was... different about him. About his energy. And, most of all, I could tell he was in danger of meeting the same fate that my family had.

And in that moment, I felt a spark in me like never before. I wanted to help that boy. I wanted to use my powers – the powers that had cost my parents and siblings their lives – to save another's.

Leaping forward from behind the tree, Destiny ran over to the two men and held her arms out – ragged clothing swaying, and frightened eyes flaring with fire. "Stop! Leave him alone!"

At first the two human men simply stared back in mixed surprise and dismissal, turning to face her with their swords raised, but then it happened – a burst of wild, forceful energy shot out of Destiny's body, and they were flung back – crashing into the trees nearby with a great slam, and appearing to fall unconscious.

Breathing hard, Destiny stared after them for a few long moments, before turning around and stepping over to the kneeling boy. He was still holding the cloth to his face. "Come on, let's get out of here."

The boy shook his head. "I... can't go back home."

Destiny dipped her chin sincerely. "You don't have to. You can stay with me."

For a long moment the boy looked up at Destiny, staring at her with his eyes half visible through the cloth he was holding to his face. Then he nodded.

Yuuto and I travelled alone for what felt like months – hopping between small villages and forests until we arrived at the foot of the Penlight Castle. It was there that we met Mase and Ika, who were the children of nobles, and saw us taken in first for accommodation and caretaking, and then to be trained as squires for the domain's king – King Aldrich.

I hid my powers, at first, and so did Yuuto – terrified that we would be thrown from our new home or put down for the safety of the kingdom. But when I was eventually discovered... it came about that the others had powers too. That I was not alone after all. The Penlight Kingdom did not understand our abilities, sure, but they did not hate them, either.

As such, I grew in the king's trust and in his service, and when he grew old, he turned to me and confessed his lack of heir – that he saw no other better to lead his domain, continue his legacy, than I.

From that day, I vowed to protect all of Penlight with my heart and soul. To Uphold justice, righteousness, and protection for all those who live in the kingdom, and to use my powers – the powers that saw my family killed – for the good of all, and to shape those powers of my kin in magic.

I'll never forget my family. Or my old name. But more important now is who I have become, the purpose I must serve... and what that means for you, Harmony. Helping you follow in my footsteps.

Destiny's voice eventually faded to silence, and Harmony's focus slowly came back to the damaged, debris-strewn training yard around her. *She lost... everything. And yet she remained strong. She learnt to control her powers for good. Can I... still do that, even after all this?*

Moving for the first time in what felt like a lifespan, Destiny stood, took a sidelong glance at Irin's motionless body, and breathed a deep, heavy sigh. "After all these years..."

Then she looked back to the kneeling, broken cat before her, and shook her head. "I won't kill you, Harmony. Despite what just happened, I feel you can grow stronger and do better. Irin... she was strong too, but she made her choice. She let her focus blur her reason and heart. That is as much her fault as it is yours, Harmony. This is our burden to carry, as those with gifts."

Harmony nodded, but she was hardly listening for the tears falling from her eyes. *I just want to see Umi...*

Stepping forward almost symbolically, Destiny extended one long, graceful arm. "Let's get you patched up, and return you home to your father.

"No. I want to stay with Umi. I... live with her now," Harmony responded. She couldn't say why, not out loud – she could only hope that the queen... that no one would ever find out. She knew for one that she herself would never return to that house.

Destiny paused for a moment, before nodding in return. "I understand. I see your mind, Harmony. But know this. This does not have to be the end. We will work, fight, and grow together."

"For ourselves, for Irin, for all those like us... for the Penlight Kingdom."

An hour or so later, Umi was standing by the door of her apartment with her coat on – expression worried, and feet posed to start walking through the door and out in search of her two friends. She'd been distressed for hours now, wondering where they'd gone.

Just as she made the final decision to walk out and start looking, however, there was a twist of dark light just to her side, and she wheeled about to see a ragged, bandaged Harmony appear in the corner of the room with a tearful expression on her face.

"Harmony?" The opossum ran over – almost wrapping the cat up in a hug, but then stopping short in realization after glancing down at the bandages once more. "You scared the life straight out of me... where did you and Irin go? What happened?"

Slowly, deeply, with the distress on her face turning to stony resignation, Harmony exhaled. "Irin and I went to the castle to fight Upholder."

Umi gasped. "What? Why would you do that? What happened – are you okay? Where is Irin?"

Harmony didn't respond, simply standing still with her arms limp by her sides.

"Harmony... please tell me." Umi held her firmly at arms' length. "Is Irin okay?"

The world stopped for a long, painful moment, as Harmony was forced to reckon with what she was going to have to say next. The image of Irin's last smile flashed before her eyes, and when she did open her lips, it was only with the greatest effort.

"She was... killed by Upholder. It's my fault she's gone. She followed me all the way through. I should've protected her better..."

Something in Umi's gaze broke. At first she simply stared back, but then she shook her head in disbelief. "That's... Why? What did you..."

She took a step back. "Why did things have to be like this?"

Harmony bowed her head in shame. *I don't want to loser her. Not her too.* "I... lost control. I just wanted to know the truth about my mother. And we fought her. Til Irin... fell."

Tears began to fall from Harmony's eyes in thick rivers, and for a long moment the two stood there in silence, before Umi came closer again and brushed her thumb across the cat girl's cheek. "That she's gone... I can't even begin to..."

She gave a heavy gulp. "But right now... I'm just glad that you're here. At least. You could be gone too. And that..."

One more step closer. "I couldn't live without you. the thought of losing you..."

Harmony raised her head just in time to see Umi leaning in – and to catch her lips with her own.

They were both crying, at first – which made for somewhat of an awkward kiss – but before long the flow stopped, and they stopped thinking altogether.

Harmony took from the relentless pain in her head, body, and heart in the comfort of Umi's closeness, and the hope that something might still lie before her.

— • —

EPILOGUE

Months passed in the territories of the Penlight Kingdom – the Queen and Kijury had their marriage, winter approached, and with it, both nature and the farmspeople that worked it slowly entered a state of calm and hibernation.

Although she continued to train and refine her control of her skills for as long as she could, soon the signs and toll of her pregnancy became undeniable, and she too retreated to wait out the coldest time of the year in peace. At the behest and grace of the queen – Destiny – Harmony and Umi were granted a house in the core ring of the city, and took up residence there together – dedication to one another only cemented by everything they had endured, and lost, together.

The birth drew nearer and nearer, and in the meantime Harmony could do little but rest and wait for the day itself, but there was one occasion that they still had on the calendar beforehand. The queen had invited both Harmony and Umi to the palace – although she hadn't given any clue as to why in her letter.

Harmony was terribly nervous about the idea – it would be the first time that she would return there after... what had happened. But she was also curious to see what the queen had in mind, and so, she and Umi agreed to attend.

On the day of the event, Harmony was sitting already dressed on the couch waiting to leave, and her ears perked up as she heard someone coming down the stairs – looking over to see her partner walk down the stairs in a simple, yellow dress set.

"How are my two favorite cats in the world doing?" She walked over to the couch, sitting next to Harmony with a smile.

Harmony purred as the opossum put her hand on her stomach, rubbing along it gently. "Just fine, love." The cat chuckled gently, and kissed Umi on the lips. "We can leave now, if you'd like."

"Mmh, just one more moment." Umi leant into the kiss wordlessly for a few long, long heartbeats before pulling back with a shy smile. "Alright. Now let's see what Upholder wants."

Harmony carefully stood up, taking Umi's paw with a smile before closing her eyes, summoning her powers, and vanishing them both into a burst of dark energy. It'd been a while since she'd used this.

A few disorientating seconds later and they appeared in the opening hall to the palace – deeply familiar stone and banners all around them. Moving forward arm in arm, they emerged out into the throne room itself, where they found Destiny sat on her throne, the knights of the Penlight – Mase, Mystic, Ika, and Yuuto – stood to either side of the space, and Kijury behind the queen.

"What's all of this about?" Harmony questioned, chuckling.

Standing from her throne, Destiny walked up to the women with a smile. "Welcome, you two. Thank you for attending, I know it must be tiring for you, so I will make things short, in the interest of preserving your time and energy."

She bowed her head. "It is with great honor, gratitude, and respect that I note your service to myself and the kingdom – both in apprehending Illusionary and bringing him to justice for his crimes, and the years of training that you have dedicated to using your powers for the good of our people."

Harmony's jaw fell. "Hold on... don't tell me..."

Destiny chuckled, nodding. "That's right, Harmony. Your training is complete, thanks to my dear Kijury, and as of now, I would like to anoint both yourself and Umi as knights of Penlight. Congratulations."

Both Harmony and Umi gasped, and clasped one another's paws harder than ever.

Destiny bowed her shoulders, and raised both her arms to place one paw upon each woman's shoulder. "I'm so proud of you two."

A loud round of applause came from the knights standing throughout the chamber, and finally moving forward, Kijury approached the two with gentle, earnest tears falling from his eyes. "I'm so proud of the both of you... Congratulations!"

"Thanks, Kijury!" Harmony and Umi spoke in unison, beaming just as brightly as the dear himself was.

Next came a seemingly endless round of shaking hands, exchanging congratulations, and even discussing their knight armor with Kijury, but amidst all of it, and despite everything that had happened over the past years... Harmony and Umi could both only feel a deep sensation of belonging – to the queen, the kingdom, and the knights that they had trained amongst for all these years, and could now consider colleagues in defending their home.

A week later, Harmony gave birth to a female savannah cub. The cub had gray fur with spots – some white, and others similar to that of a cheetah.

The evening after the birth, when the castle's midwives and healers had left their house, Harmony lay in bed cradling her thin-furred, sleeping daughter in her arms with Umi sat on the edge next to her.

"She's beautiful," the opossum spoke.

Harmony nodded in response, cradling her cub.

"What will you name her?" Umi inquired gently, smiling.

The cat didn't know how to respond, at first. And in that moment of hesitation, a voice echoed through her head. *You're worthless. To think you couldn't save your best friend, and now you have a child? You won't be able to control yourself, Harmony.*

Harmony frowned, tearing up at the thought of Irin. The funeral. The tombstone, in the forest. Everything that had let them to that moment – the decade and then some of their friendship.

"Unity Tsuki Mei."

Harmony bowed her head, tears falling down her cheeks.

Leaning in, Umi gently pulled her lover and daughter into a tight, loving embrace.

Their new lives as parents continued in a joyous, blissful haze. Harmony spent her days at home taking care of the baby, while Umi continued her service to the kingdom, and occasionally they would go for strolls together to bask in the beautiful weather. Even the dreams and the voices had mercy, and left Harmony in peace – until, at least, one night about a month after Unity's birth.

Harmony was used to being awake at this time of the night, taking care of the baby, but not finding herself standing in the middle of the nursery, unsure how she got there. The sounds of Unity crying out for attention upon noticing her mother's presence soon caused her to forget her confusion, however, and instead brought her to move towards the crib where her child lay with a reflexive, genuine smile. *Well, look who's awake!*

"My precious daughter..." Harmony reached in the crib, and gently pulled up Unity's simple, black swaddling cloth to a more comfortable, warmer position. Unity smiled at the gesture, cry turning to a giggle.

But that was when a voice spoke from just behind her ear. A smooth, well-measured voice. A familiar voice.

"Irin would love this!"

Harmony gasped out loud – hands flying back from the edge of the crib as she turned about on the spot in shock. There, not five feet away and dressed in the cloths of the church he had always worn, stood a tall, thin cheetah. Illusionary.

"Hello, Harmony." He had a deep, wicked smirk on his face.

Harmony's eyes flooded with dark energy and her hands clenched in anger, though her body was wracked with fear. "Leave. Or I'll kill you."

"You already tried that once. Now, let me see my daughter." Ignoring Harmony's presence completely, Illusionary moved closer to the crib and reached out to Unity.

Something snapped inside Harmony at that. An instinct she hadn't had to use for a long while, now. Vanishing and reappearing in the space of a split second and with only the slightest of dark puffs, she shifted behind Illusionary, grabbed his shoulder with one hand, and thrust hard into his back with her other – shattering past his spine, ribs, and out the other side. "You'll *never* touch my child."

The noise was terrible, as was the spray of gore that splattered on the wall next to the crib as a result. But what was more terrible still was the words that came next, and the familiarity of the voice they were said in.

"H-Harmony? What are you doing?"

Harmony realized immediately that that voice was no longer Illusionary's. And soon, as the form of the body in front of her began to waver and blur, it too was no longer his.

The cat woman's eyes widened in awful, sickening recognition. *Umi.*

Looking down, she could see the opossum's features, now. It was Umi's chest that her fist had broken through. It was Umi's blood coating her front. It was Umi's body falling limply to the floor in front of her.

"No... no!" Harmony exclaimed, tearing up, and crumbling to her knees. "*Not again!*"

Darkness exploded out of her. All was nothing.

Harmony jolted awake – panting, and darting her head to and fro urgently. Slowly, she began to relax. Umi was leaning against her shoulder with her eyes opened and a concerned, puzzled expression, and Unity was nowhere to be seen – likely still resting in her crib in the other room.

The opossum frowned, and caressed the cat's side. "Are you alright?"

Harmony chuckled nervously, righting herself in her seat and collecting herself. "Yeah... I had a weird dream."

"Would you like to share with the class, Miss Mei?" The opossum smiled, poking the cat's nose.

Harmony froze up a little in the sheets at that. She contemplated telling the truth – as brutal and terrifying as it might be – but then thought for a long, troubled moment, and sighed. "I dreamed... that the world was upside down for a day."

"Very weird indeed." Umi responded, yawning.

Head swimming with relief, but still feeling a bit nauseous and disorientated from the effects of the dream, Harmony stood up from the couch, stretched a bit, and turned back about with a nod. "I think... I need some fresh air. I might go for a walk in the forest for a moment, just to freshen up."

The opossum smiled up at her, before yawning loudly. "Mmh, but I'm so tired. Don't let me stop you, though – I'll follow after in a bit."

Harmony smiled back, and leant back in to give Umi a kiss. "Perfect!"

Appearing in a light-bending twist of her magic, Harmony appeared at the entrance of the Penlight Forest – dark power fading from her arms as she entered at a steady pace, and closed her eyes. *I need... time to think. To collect my thoughts. I don't want to lose control, right now. I don't want to hurt those around me, if the voices are coming back...*

Thankfully, the early morning forest was just as peaceful and cool as she'd hoped – allowing her to walk for a few minutes and breathe in the fresh, scented air without hearing so much as an animal scampering through the undergrowth.

Eventually she came to a small, round pond, and a clearing in the way. At first she only paused her feet to glance down at the pure, dusky water, but then the rest of her body followed, and her ears were shooting up in alertness. *I feel something. Someone.*

It was hard to describe – a dark, abstract pressure like in her dreams, her nightmares, and the voices in her head. Only... it was no longer inside her.

"Come out of hiding. I can feel you." Harmony's voice echoed into the darkness.

At first there was no response whatsoever, but then – just as the cat was about to turn about and continue on her way – a black figure ran across her vision from behind a tree, and Harmony was springing back into action with a cry.

"Hey!" Harmony shouted, and began to employ a mixture of dashing and teleporting in an attempt to catch up. "Get back here!"

The cat woman chased the figure deeper into the forest by the minute – and as she did so, it seemed to be slowing down. *I'm getting closer to it!* she thought, smirking. "I'll get you!"

But then, just before she thought that she was about to be able to grasp after the figure, it was suddenly impossibly nimble again – springing upwards, and disappearing amongst the heads of the trees all around.

The cat's head whirled about, and she froze – finding herself glancing around in horror as she was surrounded by more and more identical, featureless black figures, emerging from between the trunks all around her.

Heart beating harder than ever before and legs crouching back into an unarmed fighting stance, Harmony dismissed her fear in favor of a defensive snarl. "Whoever you are – I am a Knight of Penlight. You are no match for me!"

A moment of silence passed – no response. But then, without even the slightest twitch of warning, the figures leaped all at once.

The force of the first impact was enough to send her crashing to the ground helplessly already, but although this didn't faze the cat and she prepared to blast herself back up with a burst of her dark energy, when she concentrated and pushed... no such energy came.

In the moment of her confusion, she could feel a rumbling in the ground around her, and black hands appeared from the muddy soil around her to grab at her legs with unflinching, supernatural strength – pulling her down hard into the dirt.

"H-help! Umi, please!" She cried, but then one of the hands covered her mouth, preventing her making any noise other than muffled, panicked screaming.

Even the ground beneath her was no longer solid – rather an undulating, choking mass that gripped at her limbs all at once. At first, even as her vision began to darken, she fought back with every inch of her might and every fragment of her powers, but every time she released a burst of energy, the strength only sapped further from her body – draining her more and more and more until she...

Stopped. Resisting, struggling to breathe, fighting to claw back to the surface of the all-consuming dark.

Her surrender felt so natural – giving in to and heeding the calling hammering at every inch of her brain. This darkness was familiar, after all. It was the darkness that had lived within her for her entire life. That had been picking away at her resistance for almost as long. That even now was only starting with its insidious plans.

You'll join your mother, Harmony Mei.

www.ingramcontent.com/pod-product-compliance
Lightning Source LLC
Chambersburg PA
CBHW071424300726
48976CB00004B/1236